HAVEN Falls

- SHERIDAN ANNE -

SHERIDAN ANNE

Untameable

- SHERIDAN ANNE -

Cover Design by: Sheridan Anne
Photograph: Sakkmesterke
Editing and Formatting by: Sheridan Anne
Proofreading By: Jessie Lynn

CHAPTER 1

Rivers' fist slams into Noah's jaw, sending him flying back a step as a low guttural groan pulls from deep within him. I flinch with the contact despite the fact that it's not my face. "No, no, no," I grumble to myself. Does he really have to go for his face? It's too pretty. Get him anywhere except his face. Oh, and his junk. I'd like to put that to good use later and I can't if there's a packet of frozen peas on it.

"The fuck?" Noah demands, rubbing his hand across his face as Tully and I let out frustrated sighs. I mean, how many times are we going to do this trivial shit?

Rivers' shoulders pull back, standing his ground. "You heard me," he spits. "You don't have what it takes."

"Hey," Noah's mom shouts, sticking her head around the corner, poking it out from the kitchen before walking out. "What the hell is going on in here? I told you idiots; no fighting in the house."

Naturally, both boys ignore her as they stare off, both scowling and fuming.

Violet sighs and comes to stand beside me and Tully.

"What happened now?" she questions quietly. "Did Noah finally work out that you and Rivers have been bumping uglies?"

Jaw meet floor.

I whip my head around to face the mother and daughter. Did Violet seriously just say that? "What?" I shriek while still managing not to alert the boys of our conversation as I stare down Tully. "You told your mom that?"

"First off," Tully defends, looking at me. "Of course I told her, and even if I didn't, she would have worked it out. Second," she continues, turning to her mom, "We're not bumping uglies. No plural. It happened once and it won't be happening again."

Yeah freaking right. I can't hold back my scoff which earns me a sharp glare from Tully and a knowing smirk from Violet.

"Right, so if it isn't about you two, then what's it about? Cause something big has seriously crawled up those boys' asses lately," Violet murmurs.

"Tell me about it," I grumble.

Tully scrunches up her face, deep in thought before she shakes her head. "As far as I can tell, Rivers is PMSing again. I think it's something to do with his mom, and he just happened to catch Noah on a bad day. They've been at each other's throats since the second he walked through the door. Noah could tell Rivers had a chip on his shoulder again and he wouldn't let up about it until Rivers just…snapped."

Violet lets out a sigh just as Noah charges full steam ahead into Rivers. He throws his arms out and slams his shoulder into Rivers' stomach until the two of them have left a wide Noah and Rivers size gaping hole in the living room wall.

They fall to the floor and suddenly it's on. Fists start flying as grunts are heard from deep within them.

Boys will be boys, right?

"Damn it," Violet growls, still being ignored by the boys. "I told you no fighting in the house. How am I going to explain this to your father?"

All I can do is shake my head as I watch.

Something is going on with Rivers and as far as I can tell, it's got something to do with his family. I don't know how much of that he's shared with Tully, but as for me, I'm in the dark. As much as I love Rivers and have come to know who he is, when I really think about it, he's still a stranger to me.

I know nothing of his personal life, and I haven't been able to work out if that's a good thing or not. Something tells me that the second he walks out of this house every night, darkness clouds him, and I think the reason he's not sharing that with me is because he doesn't want to bring that down on me. I want to thank him for that, but at the same time, I want to hate him for it. It makes me feel like I'm being left out of the loop.

But hell, who even knows how much he's even shared with Noah and Tully? Rivers is a mystery and I have a feeling he's someone that no one is ever going to figure out. Tully might get close, but I don't think he'll ever truly let her in.

Noah's elbow rears back and slams another hole in the wall, and to be honest, I don't even think he realizes. His fist comes forward and nails Rivers in the gut before Rivers swiftly responds with one of his own.

"Shit," Violet sighs, shocking me with her cursing. "This could go on a while. I'll go get some ice ready."

Tully presses her lips into a straight line. "I'll find the bandages."

They both scurry off and I drop down onto the couch. "And I will watch the show." With that, I prop my feet up onto the coffee table and sit back, watching these two guys beat the absolute shit out of each other.

Twenty minutes later, Noah sits against the headboard on his bed with me straddling his lap, patching up the cut above his eyebrow. "You know," I muse, "sometimes situations can be handled without using your fists."

Noah's hands fall to my waist. "I know," he says, flinching

as I clean up the cut. "He needed it though. The second he walked in he was looking for a fight."

I cock a brow. "So, you let him use you as a punching bag?"

Noah shrugs his shoulders. "Yep," he tells me. "It's better he gets it all out of his system here then go looking for trouble somewhere else."

Jesus Christ. If this is the boys fighting to let off steam, I can only imagine how it's going to go down when Noah finds out about Rivers and Tully. There will be bloodshed that day and I can honestly say that I don't want to be anywhere near them when it happens.

"You're a good friend, Noah," I murmur. "But, have you heard of this thing called a gym? If he needed to beat something up, why didn't you just take him there? He could have laid into a punching bag and saved your face."

He shakes his head, his fingers digging into my skin as I work on the cut. "Nope. Wouldn't have worked," he says. "Rivers needs the rush. He wouldn't have gotten the same satisfaction beating the crap out of a bag. He needed to feel pain, and he needed to cause it."

"So, you volunteered to be his target?"

"Yep."

"You're an idiot."

"Tell me something I don't know."

I roll my eyes and finish up working on his head before leaning into his chest. His warm arms circle me and hold me tight when I feel a rumble through his chest. "Sorry you had to see that."

"It's fine," I murmur. "I'm not going to lie. It wasn't great seeing someone hit you, but watching you fight back was the best thing I've ever watched."

"Is that why you were sitting back on the couch with your feet up? You were getting hot? You were looking a little flushed."

I can't see his face, but I can certainly picture the cocky, too sure of himself smirk on his lips. I let out a breath and try to reign in my grin, but let's face it; I can't. He's right…as usual. Noah Cage has an effect on my body that I simply can't control. Maybe it's the tattoos…or maybe it's the heart beneath.

I let out a sigh. As much as I want to go where he's trying to take this right now, I can't; my mind is too heavy. "What's going on with him?" I ask, slipping my hand under his shirt and sliding it up until it hovers over his beating heart.

The feel of his skin under mine is incredible, but when his fingers trail up my back and push into my hair, holding me to him, well, that's so much better. Noah's silent for a moment and I try to work out if he's figuring out a way to avoid the topic, searching for what to say, or trying to decipher how to word something that isn't my business. "Honestly," he tells me. "I haven't got a fucking clue."

I glance up at him and one look into those green eyes tells me that this is his truth and something else tells me that it really fucking bothers him. "Tully thinks it's got something to do with his mom."

Noah sighs. "It's always his mom."

"What's going on with her? I've never heard him talk about her before."

"Exactly," he grunts. "He never talks about her. I think things are messed up there, but I couldn't tell you what. I've never met her before."

"What?" I grunt. "How have you never met her? You guys have been friends for years."

"I know," he scoffs, shrugging his shoulders. "We're guys; fucked up guys. We bonded over kicking peoples' asses and drawing blood, not chatting about our family issues."

"Are you trying to make yourself sound tough?" I laugh.

"Please," he scoffs. "I don't need to make myself look tough. You already believe it."

"Cocky prick."

"Princess."

I shake my head and let out a sigh. He and I both know that I'm the furthest thing from a princess. Tully, well that's a different story. "So, he hasn't said anything to you?"

A grin rips across his handsome face as he looks down at me. "Have you met the guy? Do you really get the impression that he's the type to sit around sharing his feelings?"

I can't help but smirk at the absurdity of it as an image of Rivers sitting down for high tea, talking about his day sails through my mind. "No," I laugh. "I guess not."

"Exactly," he says, his hand coming around to my chin and tilting it up towards his. "Now, tell me," he smiles against my lips. "Do you have any other tricks to make me feel better?"

Do I ever!

My lips move against his as I melt into him. I freaking love this. Being with Noah has been nothing short of a wild ride and I wouldn't change it for anything. We've certainly had some ups and downs over the past few months, but in short, they've been amazing.

Falling in love for the first time has been a bit of a rocky journey. It was my first time, how was I supposed to understand what I was feeling? But having a guy like Noah along for the ride...damn. I'm a lucky girl. I couldn't possibly imagine that it's like this for everyone.

Noah is a beast. He's kind, caring, sexy as hell, and downright terrifying if he needs to be. What can I say? He's the whole damn package. All he needs now is a motorcycle and a leather jacket.

I pull back from his lips before I get completely lost in a world of Noah. "We can't," I grumble, struggling to remove myself from him.

"Hell yeah, we can," he tells me, pulling me back in.

I place my hands down on his chest and pull away once again. "No," I all but cry, hating the distance I have to put between us, but let's face it, if I don't, this is where we'll stay for the rest of the day. Besides, there's a massive hole in

Violet's wall that needs to be fixed.

"Come on, Spitfire," he groans, and I swear, if I look close enough, I could almost say that he's pouting…just a little.

I shake my head. "You need to go and check that Rivers isn't out there playing with his pocketknife, just waiting for you to walk by. Then you need to fix the wall."

"The wall?" he grunts, his brows drawing down.

"Yeah, the massive hole you put in your mother's wall. She wasn't too impressed with it."

"Shit. Did we really?" he laughs. "I didn't even notice."

"Are you kidding me?" I grin as I climb off his lap and pull him up behind me. "You practically threw Rivers through the whole damn thing. I was worried I was going to have to take my viewing party outside. How could you not notice that? You put your elbow through it too."

He looks down at his elbow, twisting it around so he can see it properly, and sure enough, there's dried blood all over it, but naturally, he couldn't give a shit. Noah shrugs his shoulder. "Oh well. It wasn't my back that went through it."

I shake my head. These damn, infuriating boys!

"Come on," I tell him. "Let's get this over and done with so you can take advantage of me."

His eyes light up in excitement. "Fucking deal."

Noah's fingers weave through mine and I walk out the door, dragging him behind me, despite him pulling back on my arm, more than reluctant to come out here.

He groans behind me but I ignore it as the conversation from the living room draws every ounce of my attention.

"Just…fuck, Rivers," Tully groans.

I peek around the corner to find Tully sitting on the edge of the coffee table trying her hardest to put an ice pack on Rivers' ribs as he keeps swatting her away. "Babe, stop," he tells her.

Tully huffs as she watches the man who's completely captured her while nothing but frustrations rolls of her.

"Damn it, Rivers. Stop being such a fucking pussy. You have to ice it or it'll get worse. I'm just trying to help. Stop pushing me away."

He sits up a little straighter, grabbing the ice pack from her hand and tossing it in her lap. "I don't need your fucking help."

Oh shit.

Noah tenses behind me and we find ourselves pausing in the hallway, wondering how this is going to play out. No doubt that would have cut her on a level that only Rivers is capable of. Usually, nothing gets to Tully. She's as fierce as they come, but where Rivers is concerned, she has a weakness.

Tully pushes to her feet. "For fuck's sake," she yells at him before throwing the ice pack at him with probably a little too much force. "Screw you. Bruise for all I care."

With that, she grabs her jacket off the edge of the couch and storms out the front door, pinching her keys off the entryway table on her way. Rivers watches her leave with a deflated sigh and I press my lips together watching the scene before me. Did he really have to do that? After all the pain he's already caused to her poor heart?

"Seriously?" Noah grunts behind me, pushing me up the hallway to get my feet moving again. "Did you really have to do that? She was just trying to help."

"I don't need her help," Rivers murmurs, looking pissed off with himself. Probably hating that he just pushed her away again, knowing how much it would have hurt.

"You owe her a fucking apology," Noah tells him.

Rivers lets out a strained breath. "I know. I will. I just," his eyes flick up to ours before focusing on the door she just walked out of. "I don't like her seeing me like this."

I step forward. "You're not indestructible," I tell him. "She knows that, and I'm sure as hell she's seen you a lot worse than this."

Rivers groans as Noah steps in behind me and looks over

him. "You all good though? All out of your system now?"

"Yeah," he sighs, pushing up to his feet with a cringe, holding his ribs as though they're about to fall out of his body. "Sorry 'bout your eye."

"It's cool," Noah says, his eyes focusing on Rivers' ribs just as mine are. And apparently, just like that, the boys are back to their usual best friend status. I mean, if they were chicks, this would be going down very differently. Noah squeezes my waist. "It turns Henley on. It'll get me laid later."

I slam my elbow back into Noah's stomach, despite the fact that it's probably covered in bruises. I step forward into Rivers. "Show me," I tell him. He scoffs down at me, but I hold my ground. "Now, Rivers," I say, "or I'm telling Violet they're broken."

"Shit," he groans before reaching the back of his shirt and shrugging out of it. Rivers turns to the side, lifting his arm to give me a better look. I can't help but press my fingers across the harsh bruising that's already appearing.

"Fuck," Noah grunts. "Sorry man. I'll get the tape."

Noah disappears into the kitchen as I feel across Rivers ribs making sure nothing's broken. "Did this happen when you went through the wall?" I ask.

"Yeah, I think so," he murmurs. "Didn't help that the fucker nailed me there right after."

"You brought it on yourself," I remind him. "If you left your bad attitude at the door and didn't come here searching for a fight then you'd probably be kicking back right now, staring and drooling over Tully while pretending she doesn't exist."

"I don't need a lecture from you right now."

I press a little harder and get a disgusting amount of satisfaction out of the hiss that sails out of him. "Well, you're going to fucking hear one," I tell him a little more firmly. "You hurt my boyfriend and now you've hurt my best friend, again. This shit has to stop."

I can practically hear his eyes roll.

I grab the discarded ice pack and slap it against his skin, grinning at the way he tries to pull away from it. After all, I didn't bother wrapping it in a paper towel the way Tully had. Screw that shit. Rivers needs tough love right now, not the bullshit tending to his every need that Tully would have given him had he allowed her the chance.

Nope. Fuck that. It kind of makes me glad that Noah did a little damage.

Noah comes striding back in the room with the tape in his hands and he tosses it across to me while he stops to inspect the hole in the wall. I remove the ice pack and start taping Rivers up as Noah whistles. "We're going to have to fix this before dad gets home."

"Yep," Rivers agrees as I finish off with the tape and shove his shirt back into his hands.

"Do you need a number for a carpenter?" I ask, pulling out my phone.

"Nah," Noah grumbles as Rivers pulls his shirt back on and wraps the ice pack with the discarded paper towel. "We've put so many fucking holes in walls that we had to learn how to patch it ourselves. It was getting too expensive," he laughs. "Besides, it's not too hard."

"So, what now then?" I ask as Rivers presses the ice pack back to his sore ribs.

"Now, we go down to the hardware store."

CHAPTER 2

A weight crushes down on my chest and I gasp for breath as my eyes flick open in panic. "Fuck," I grunt out as I find Aria staring down at me while busily trying to squish my boobs back into my body. I mean, that's not how it works. "Get off me, Squirt."

She giggles as though watching me struggle to breathe is the funniest thing she's ever seen, but thankfully, slides off me and crashes down onto the pillow beside me. "I'm hungry."

"You're always hungry," I grumble, wishing the sun would disappear for a while longer. Noah only dropped me home a few hours ago which is probably a bit stupid on our part, seeing as though it's a Monday morning. "What's the time?"

She shrugs her shoulders and I curse myself out. She's only five. What was I thinking asking her the time? She can't read the clock yet.

I reach over her and grab my phone off my bedside table to check the time. "Damn it," I moan under my breath, realizing it's not even six yet. "Can't I sleep a little while longer?"

"But I'm hungry now," she whines. "I tried to make my breakfast but it was too hard."

Oh no. "What did you try to make?"

"Cereal."

"Ok…and which part was too hard?"

Her eyes cut away from mine with nothing but guilt shining back through them. "The milk was too heavy and when I poured…"

"Go on."

She holds up her hands to demonstrate what happened and from what I can tell as she poured, she couldn't stop it fast enough, telling me there's a pool of milk in the kitchen to clean up. I let out a sigh as I curse dad for having a job today. "Fine," I groan. "Just let me pee first and then we'll clean it all up."

She beams back at me before bouncing off my bed with unbelievable amounts of energy. I mean, thank God it's a school day. I couldn't handle that all day considering I've hardly had any sleep.

Aria practically pulls me from my bed and drags me down the hallway. She stops at the bathroom door and no doubt listens to me pee but has patience on her side today as she doesn't come right on in with me. You know, apart from the whole dragging me out of bed before six in the morning thing.

I deal with business and before I know it, Aria's dragging me the rest of the way down the hallway towards the kitchen. "How bad is it?" I ask, trying to prepare myself.

"It's bad," she chuckles to herself.

"Is there any milk left?" Aria shakes her head. "I guess I won't be making cereal then," I murmur. "What should I make?"

Her little eyes brighten up at the thought of having options and I'm struck for the millionth time at how the little things in life that I so easily take for granted are such a big deal for her. She's probably never been offered options before and it breaks me every time I'm reminded of it.

"Ummmmmmmmmm," she draws out. "Can I have pancakes and cupcakes?"

I laugh out. "You can have pancakes. There's no way I'm baking cupcakes at this time of the morning." As her face falls, I find myself desperate to make it right. "How about this?" I tell her. "If you're a good girl for me this morning, we can stop by the bakery on the way to school and get you something special for your lunch."

"Really?" she questions, jumping up and down as we turn into the kitchen.

"Of cour-"

Oh, dear lord. This mess!

There's milk dripping off the bench, on to the old floors and making a little pool that has her cheerios floating on top. The box of cereal was knocked over in the process and cheerios spread from one end of the kitchen to the other. I don't understand how it's physically possible for one little girl to make such a mess while trying to make a bowl of cereal.

This is the reason I don't want a teen pregnancy. I couldn't handle being in charge of this kind of destruction every day. I mean, God knows I love my little sister, but she's the best tool to convince teens to use contraception.

I stand on the spot, still as a statue as I try to make a game plan. "Right," I tell her. "You go get the broom and sort out the cheerios while I work on the milk. As soon as that's done, we make pancakes, but it's going to have to be a packet mix because unfortunately, we're now out of milk."

She grins up at me as innocently as possible.

Damn it. How could I be cranky at that face?

As my eyes rake over the kitchen, I take in the familiar note sitting on the bench with a fifty dollar note on top. Instincts have me moving towards it.

I scoop the note up off the table and hold it up, letting

the milk drip off the edge and hope I can still read the blurry, milk destroyed words.

Squish & Squirt,
I'll be gone for the night and hopefully back before school drop off
tomorrow morning.
There's enough food in the fridge to feed an army.
Be safe and call me if you need anything.
Squish - Don't be an asshole to your sister. Read her as many bedtime
stories as she wants!
Squirt – I know you can't read but I'm trusting your big sister to let
you know that you'll be safe with her and to be a good girl in class. I
don't want any more calls from your teacher!
Be good.
Love you both.
Dad.

Dad left early this morning, probably shortly after I got home actually, so let's hope he didn't realize how late I'd gotten in. Since he didn't call me out in his note, I'd say I'm in the clear.

This has become our new normal. As hard as it is, dad still needs to work and now that I'm apparently old enough to be responsible, that means I need to be a little more helpful. Dad needs to work more now than ever as our bills just suddenly doubled. He does as many jobs as he can while trying to remain as close to home as possible.

I keep thinking about getting myself a job to help out where I can, but the only times I'll be able to work are after school and weekends which is usually when I have Aria with me. It's a lose/lose situation, but dad assures me it's better if I'm home with her.

I move the cash away from the spilled milk and stick it to the fridge, under a magnet. There's no more hiding cash away in my old jewelry box, not anymore. Every cent counts now, and here on the fridge, it won't get lost. I can cook us something for dinner to avoid spending it, besides, the gas bill is due soon and we need to keep on top of it as dad has a habit of forgetting due dates. What the hell would he do without me?

Aria and I get to work scrubbing the kitchen and within ten minutes, it's squeaky clean. Actually, that's probably too much of an exaggeration. It's...clean enough to be able to cook in so naturally, that's exactly what we do.

Pancake mix goes everywhere and I'm glad we have so much time before having to head out for school because the kitchen is going to need a second scrub once we're done with it, and then Aria will probably need a scrub too.

Aria sits up at the table and devours her breakfast in the blink of an eye before reaching across and stealing half of mine.

I roll my eyes as I watch her. She's such a terror.

After breakfast, I force her to go and have a shower despite her endless whining that '*SpongeBob Square Pants*' is starting soon. I seriously don't understand her obsession with that show. It drives me insane.

Somehow, she gets through a shower and even lets me wash her hair. Half an hour later, I sit down on the couch with Aria sitting in front of me on the floor. I brush through her long blonde hair as she cheers when another episode comes on.

Kill me now.

It's not long before I doze off on the couch for a well needed sleep with Aria zoned out in the land of all things '*SpongeBob*'.

The sound of her giggles wakes me and my eyes instantly fly up to the clock on the wall. "Crap, it's nearly time to go," I shriek, flying up to my feet. "Why didn't you wake me?"

Aria doesn't even blink and it's like she's zombified by the TV. I swear, she probably doesn't even realize I'm still here. I roll my eyes. I doubt I'm going to be blessed with a response from her.

With her hair, breakfast, and shower already done, I can mostly concentrate on getting myself ready for the day. At least I was able to get a bit more sleep before having to spend the day at school.

I hurry down to my room and throw on a pair of ripped jeans and a black shirt before pulling on my combat boots. Looking in the mirror, I gasp at the sight before me. This simply won't do. I run my fingers through my hair and mess it around a little to give me that 'I don't give a shit about it' vibe which seems to be my motto for life, before tracing a little eyeliner around my eyes and adding some mascara just because I can.

I hardly ever wear makeup anymore and the look on Noah's face is fucking priceless when I do. He loves when I wear mascara. I think it has something to do with the way it makes my blue eyes stand out. I don't know, but he always seems to kiss me a little longer when I'm wearing it, and the way he seems to always be hard when he's pushing up against me makes it so damn worth it. Knowing something so simple turns him on is like a power every woman should possess. Besides, why shouldn't I wear it if he likes it so much? Especially if it means a little extra special attention from a guy who could make me cum just from a simple wink.

Hell to the yes, please.

How did I get so damn lucky?

I hurry out of my room, making sure to grab my phone and bag on the way before heading for the front door. "Right, Squirt. TV off. We have to go."

I stand at the door waiting as she slowly gets up and turns off the TV. She grabs her school bag off the floor, slips her shoes on, and finally walks towards me.

Only she stops. "I need to poop."

I let out a sigh. "Of course you do."

I take her bag from her and head outside to warm up the truck while she goes to the bathroom. Don't ask me why she didn't go before. It completely baffles me, but it's my fault.

If I was on the ball, I would have remembered to tell her to go earlier, but silly me, I fell asleep instead.

Oh well, I'd take being a few minutes late a million times over if it meant a few hours of extra sleep.

I make my way out to the truck and jam the key in the side to unlock it because well, asking for an automatic lock on this old girl is like seeing a caveman walking around with an iPhone. It's just never going to happen, not on this old truck.

I throw Aria's school bag in the back seat before noticing my neighbor, Rocko, staring at me. A shudder runs through me and we find ourselves in some kind of staring competition. Surely, he must notice the set of balls I've been growing over the past few weeks because there's no way in hell I'm about to back down.

Rocko quirks a brow, presses his lips into a thin line as though he's deep in thought, and nods his head before dropping down into his car and peeling out of his drive.

Well, that was fucking weird. Usually, I have to shoo him away and say some kind of awful thing to get rid of him, but today...I don't know, it was almost like he just pulled a bit of respect out of his ass and thrust it upon me. I don't really know how I feel about that, but it's better than having his scowl hitting me every time I walk out of the house.

He's such a freaking weirdo. There're plenty of rumors going around about him. Some girls say he likes to get a little handsy and forceful at parties while other rumors say that he's the guy responsible for burning down the bleachers at the old football field at school. I don't know if any of it is true as I've never bothered to get to know the guy, not even when Jackson was friends with him, but from the ever-present scowl on his face, I'd dare say that most of it is true.

He's not a good guy and I don't have the need within me to figure out why. He's a book that I'll happily keep closed, now and forever.

I try to forget about it and climb up into the truck. I leave the door wide open in case Aria needs me inside and turn the key with a deep twinge in my gut. There's usually about a fifty/fifty chance that the truck won't start. It never bothered me too much before as it's only a short ten minute walk to school, but with Aria at the elementary school, it turns into a massive forty minute hike that I'm simply not in the mood for today. I can't count how many lunchtime detentions I've been getting for being late, but one call from dad to the principal and we got that shit straightened right out.

Noah always tells me to call him when shit like that happens and as much as I love him for the offer, it's too much effort. We'd have to wait around for him to get here and then switch the carseat over to his car which isn't exactly easy, and then get Ari to school. We almost always end up late anyway.

But today, the truck is as happy as a pig in mud.

I leave the truck running and go back to the door.

Aria is only a few more moments and I lock the door behind her before we trudge up to the truck and climb in. She gets buckled and before I know it, I'm dropping her off at the door and beaming back at her as she gives me a huge smile.

She absolutely adores going to big girl school. She wasn't enrolled before and it's been a bit of work catching her up to the other kids her age. In fact, there's still a bit of work to go. She never went to daycare and hasn't had someone sitting by her side teaching her how to count or doing the alphabet. After all, mom was too busy getting high or stoned. Everything Aria knows, she's learned from watching TV. It's heartbreaking, but me and dad are convinced that with the help from the school and community activities, we can get her the education that she deserves.

I climb back up into the truck and haul ass to Haven Falls Private with just moments to spare before the bell sounds. I pull up next to Noah's Camaro and grin as I realize he's waited for me with Rivers, though naturally, where Rivers is,

Tully isn't.

Noah walks around to my side as I cut the engine and opens the door for me. As I jump down, he steadies me with his hands on my waist before pressing a kiss to my lips. "You look stressed out," he murmurs, pushing a golden lock of hair back behind my ear.

"You could say that," I laugh. "Ari kept me on my toes this morning."

He grins back at me. "I should have known," he says, reaching around me to grab my bag from the truck. "You ready for this?"

I ignore his questions, reaching up to stroke my fingers across his brow. "You know, I think you were right," I tell him. "I'm really digging this scar."

A grin brightens his face. "I fucking knew it, Spitfire."

I turn to Rivers and narrow my eyes. "As for you, Fucker. Lay your hands on my man again and I'll be forced to take you out."

"Yeah right," Rivers scoffs. "I'd like to see you try."

I turn to look up at the school and just like every day since I took Monica down two weeks ago, the students of Haven Falls Private are already heading my way.

I pull my game face on, straighten my back and raise my shoulders.

Your Queen is here, Haven Falls.

CHAPTER 3

A coffee is thrust into my hand by some junior I've never met as some random cheerleader steps up beside me, not talking but just walking as though she belongs there. I stop in the middle of the hallway, students all around me staring on.

The cheerleader's face falls as fear flashes behind her eyes.

I'm the new queen here. I never intended to be, it just kind of fell in my lap after I took out Monica. I already had Candice in my back pocket and without Monica leading all the sheep astray, they needed someone else to worship.

I like to say it's because I'm Noah's girlfriend, but Noah, Tully, and Rivers assures me it's not. They think it's because I'm the only chick in school who has enough balls to put bitches in their place. I'm not afraid of a fight and after years of watching me get back up every time someone knocked me down, they came to the conclusion that I'm someone worth following.

What a fucking joke, right? If only they knew the real me, they'd want to keep far enough away to avoid needing a facial reconstruction.

I don't particularly agree with their judgment. I'm just trying to get through my day without tripping and landing face first in a pile of dog shit. The rest of the school though, they have different plans for me.

I must admit, being the queen of the school does come with its perks. After falling asleep this morning, I didn't get a chance to grab a coffee, yet here it is, waiting, toasty warm in my hands. I have girls fawning over my every need and it's a damn good change of pace.

The cheerleader standing before me shrinks back as I narrow my eyes on her, keeping a straight face despite the fact that I want nothing more than to laugh at the way she reacts to me. It's funny - they want to be near me, want my protection because I seem to act first and ask questions later, but when it comes down to it, they're all terrified of me proving once and for all that they don't have what it takes to walk by my side.

That's exactly why I have my pack. They're the only people in Haven Falls with a backbone strong enough to be my people. I'm so damn happy I found them.

"Can I help you?" I ask the cheerleader, pulling out my 'boss bitch' tone.

"I...I just," she stammers before falling silent.

"That's what I thought," I grunt. "Now, hurry along." She hesitates a moment and I try my hardest to reign in my inner bitch, but no, she's shining bright today.

I step into the cheerleader, crowding her into the locker. "Let me guess," I start as she swallows back fear while the rest of the hallway watches on. "Some bitch wronged you and you want to look like king fucking shit by walking at my side, making out like you have my protection instead of growing a pair of balls and asking me directly, or better yet, dealing with your shit by yourself."

Her eyes widen in shock as though she's surprised that I knew what she wanted, but how could I not? All these girls are the same. They never spoke a word to me before now, but all of a sudden, they think they deserve a space at my side. Yeah fucking right. My protection is earned, not handed out to anyone who will take it. I mean, where did all the backbones go? Tully and I couldn't possibly be the only chicks around here with balls of steel.

"It's just…" the cheerleader stutters.

"No, honey," I say shaking my head. "That isn't how this works. What did you think? That I was going to bend over backward and take care of your shit because you're too fucking scared to do it yourself? No. No way in hell. Go and handle your own shit. You're fucking nothing. You're weak. Bitches like you who can't stand up for themselves and face their own demons are nothing. You don't deserve the protection of my pack, now shoo. Get the fuck out of here."

"But, I…I thought we could be friends?"

Ha. Liar.

"What?" I boom out. "Friends? Are you kidding me? Tell me, why now? Why be my friend now after going to school with me for so long? All of a sudden, I'm the fucking Queen around here and now you want to be my friend. Huh, funny," I grin down at her, resisting a scoff. "I see right through you and let me tell you, it's freaking embarrassing."

She starts shaking her head. "No, no. That's not what I…"

"That's not what you meant?" I question. "Have I got that wrong? You don't want to be my friend? So, if you're not looking for my protection, you don't want to be friends, and considering you're a cheerleader, you're not after the popularity boost, then what is it? Oh, maybe you're just after Noah?"

"No," she rushes out, eyes even wider.

I step further into her, going with it despite the fact that I was right all along. She's after my protection from some bitch who's probably even weaker than her but screwing with her just seems a little too much fun for me to pass up on my Monday morning. "That's it, isn't it? You think you could worm your way into my life, maybe get close enough that I'll even invite you over. What then? You wait until my back is turned and make your move? It won't work, honey," I whisper. "He's not interested in trash like you."

"No, I swear," she cowers. "I don't want him. I promise, I just..."

I let out a sigh and reach for her before pulling her into the locker where our conversation can be a little more private. "Be fucking real," I demand, having enough of this shit. "Stop cowering and stand the fuck up for what you want. How the hell are you going to get anywhere in life if you can't even find the strength to ask someone for help? What's your name?"

"Stephanie."

"Right, Stephanie. Go and grow a pair of balls and leave me the hell alone. I'm not about to fight your fight. That doesn't solve anything except for making me look even more badass than I already am. You come out looking weak and whoever the fuck you want me to take down comes out looking like a fool. Take the fucking high road and handle your shit yourself. If not, she's just going to keep coming back. Got it?"

Her head bobbles around and I see the relief leave her, probably because she's narrowly escaped one hell of an ass whooping. She stands there staring at me. "Shoo, Stephanie," I tell her, losing my patience.

As if not even realizing what she was doing, she jumps into action and scrambles away, leaving me standing by some random locker with a room full of eyes still on me. "Scram," I tell them trying not to grin at the way they all run away.

I've said it before and I'll say it again, being the Queen around here certainly has its perks.

I hold power within the ranks here. I don't get elbowed in the hallways and I don't have random cheerleaders backing me into corners to put in my place. Not that they were ever able to actually put me in my place, but they certainly tried.

What I say matters now and I have to admit, it's a weird feeling to get used to. I'm so used to being the black sheep around here. I'm the girl who got picked on, joked about, and taunted with every step I took, but not anymore. It's crazy being the girl that everyone else wants to either be or be with. It's the kind of attention other girls fight for, but not me. I want nothing more than to get rid of it, but it's simply not happening.

I'd like to be one of those girls who makes a difference. You know, use this newfound popularity for good instead of evil, but it's hard. When everyone is suddenly wanting to be your friend for their own selfish reasons and every person you talk to is either terrified of you or being fake, it's hard to remember who the fuck you are.

"What the hell was that about?" Tully questions ripping me out of my inner thoughts as she comes to join me by my locker.

My eyes search the long hallway for Noah, finding him at the opposite end, jamming shit into his locker with Rivers leaning up against the one beside him, completely oblivious to the cranky girl standing behind him, needing to use it before the bell rings.

"Nothing," I grumble, opening my locker and jamming my bag and jacket inside with a little more force than necessary. "Just another person trying to use me to get herself ahead."

Tully sighs and gives me a tight-lipped smile. "You'll get used to it," she says. I desperately want to believe her, after all, she's been in my position ever since she could walk. She's always been the popular girl and being Noah's twin sister, it's like being the popular girl on steroids. Their popularity astounds me. It's seriously ridiculous. I don't know how they put up with it.

"I seriously doubt that," I tell her with a groan. "I mean, why can't girls just do shit for themselves? Surely they know that trying to get me to fight their battles is a lost cause."

"You'd think," she laughs. "Girls are bitches and they always have an ulterior motive. The trick is figuring out what it is before they get the best of you."

"Or you can do what I do," I tell her, "and shut it down before they even have a chance to worm their way in."

"True," she says with a roll of her eyes after having seen me do just that many times over the past few weeks. I've certainly gotten good at it. "Not all girls can be like me."

"You mean horny with fucked up priorities?"

A grin rips across her face. "Exactly."

I shake my head and get the things I need for my first few classes out of my locker, knowing the bell is bound to go off any moment now. As I shut my locker, both mine and Tully's eyes instinctively trail to the opposite end of the hallway, taking in the other half of our pack.

My eyes rake over Noah and the way he carelessly leans against his locker, talking to Rivers with his hands shoved deep into his pockets has me desperate to run my hands over him. He's so fucking hot. I simply can't get over it.

His green eyes. The sharp jaw covered in a light, hot as hell stubble. His tall, wide frame. The strong muscles I know I'll find beneath his clothes. His shoulders. His smirk. His tight waist. And fuck me, the tattoos. He's simply delicious and I'm lucky as hell that I get to be the girl crawling into his bed at night.

We've been together for just over four months and every single day I find something new about him that seems to drive me a little more wild. Yesterday, I discovered that he pronounces the word slobbery wrong. He says sloppery instead of slobbery and despite the fact that I howled with laughter, I found it absolutely adorable.

I can't wait to find out what I learn about him today.

Tully though, she couldn't give a shit about her brother right now. Her eyes are all for Rivers and I'm not going to lie, watching her fight over whether to give him dreamy eyes or a scowl is pretty amusing. The fact that he hurt her wasn't too amusing though.

I hate that he hurt her and no doubt, he hates it too. They're so damn perfect together that it grates on my nerves because they're not. She's head over heels in love with the guy and I know he loves her too. But they're both complete idiots. I mean, how freaking hard can it be? If I could work it out with Noah then surely, they can too.

Rivers is convinced he's not good enough for her and I guess she'd understand that more if Rivers was willing to share a little more about himself. We don't know anything. We don't know his parents. Where he lives. What the hell he does when he's not with us. He's a closed book and he hasn't got even the slightest intention of letting any of us in.

They slept together a few weeks ago and while Tully was busy drooling about his…ahem, piercing, Rivers was busy trying to figure out the best way to tell her it was a mistake. Seeing the pain on her face absolutely gutted me. I remember how devastating it felt when Noah told me that he was going to be with Monica and that was before I'd fallen in love with him. Tully is head over freaking heels so I can only imagine how deep it cut.

At least she's finally pulled back on her whoring around. Right after he hurt her, she did everything in her power to make him jealous, and damn, it worked like a freaking charm. That was until she took it too far and actually slept with someone else. It just had to be Spencer Jones, only the biggest douchebag in Haven Falls.

Damn it, maybe I'm being a little mean. The guy certainly has a few redeeming qualities. He's a nice guy, but he always happens to be in the wrong place at the wrong time. Tully dated him last summer, I used him to forget about Noah and almost ended up taking it too far, he was the guy who offered us the joint which nearly put us in a very bad situation, and now this. I can only imagine what would happen if Noah found out about it. He's already given the guy a broken jaw and I bet he's desperate to do it again.

But…if he found out about Rivers and Tully. Damn. I don't even want to imagine what would happen there.

Blood will be spilled, hearts will shatter, and trust will be broken.

All thoughts of Tully and Noah are gone when a girl in the shortest skirt I've ever seen strides up to my guy. Her ass cheeks hang out the bottom and eyes from everywhere fall upon her creamy cheeks. Not mine though, they're focused on the manicured hand she places on Noah's chest.

It's like my eyes zone in on them like weapons of mass destruction. Does she not know what a dangerous game she's playing?

I watch as Noah glances down at the hand with amusement on his handsome face. The girl must mistake it for interest as she throws her head back and laughs at whatever he must have said.

She steps in a little closer and I cock an eyebrow. Waiting. Watching.

Noah's eyes lift to mine as the girl presses her tits into his hard chest and smiles up at him. Noah grins at me, knowing exactly how this is going to play out and heat flames within me as he winks. How can I not be used to that yet? This shit never gets old. Not with Noah.

The girl looks up at him, probably wondering why the fuck his arm hasn't circled around her waist like she's used to guys doing when she realizes his eyes aren't on her.

She looks back over her shoulder, more than ready to shoot a glare at whatever is holding his attention, but upon seeing who that glare is aimed at, she quickly falters.

Her gasp is nearly heard all the way down the opposite end of the hallway before she rips her hand away from his chest and practically launches herself across the hallway until her back is slamming into the lockers on the other side.

Her eyes never leave mine once, and to be honest, keeping a straight face that long is damn hard.

"Fuck," Tully laughs beside me, having caught every

moment of that little entertaining show. "These girls really fear you. You and him, you're like Beyoncé and Jay Z. Un-fucking-touchable."

"Damn straight," I tell her as the bell sounds loudly through the school. A devilish grin settles on my face as we start heading towards homeroom. "I'll fuck up a bitch who dares to take what belongs to me."

She rolls her eyes knowing I'm being slightly dramatic. I mean, girls have tried every day since the very first day and it's never stuck because Noah is mine just as much as I am his. He's not interested in fucking around and letting random chicks hang off him like he used to, and most of them have figured it out, but naturally, there are a few who are a little late to the party.

We walk towards the boys as they start walking toward us, both of their homerooms at the other end of the school. Noah stops just as we're about to pass, his arm shooting out and circling my waist before pulling me in hard against his chest. "You enjoyed that way too much," he tells me.

My chin raises to his and my lips hover just in front of his. "Is that a bad thing?"

"Fuck no, babe," he murmurs before gently pressing his lips to mine. "I love having a girlfriend who's a natural chick repellent."

"Same could be said for you," I tell him. I mean, guys won't even approach me out of sheer respect for Noah.

"That's got nothing to do with me, Spitfire," he chuckles. "You scare them away all on your own."

"Ha, ha. You're so funny, Noah."

"You know it," he grins, proud of his stupid joke before kissing me once again. "Try not to get yourself in detention today. I plan on taking advantage of you in the broom closet at lunch."

"Have I ever told you how romantic you are?"

He winks and with that, he heads off to homeroom, leaving me looking back over my shoulder, staring at that perfect ass of his.

CHAPTER 4

It's been a long ass day and I'm desperate to get home, but I have one more class left. My only saving grace is that it's Advanced Biology and while everyone else seems to hate it, I absolutely love it.

I don't know what it is about Biology class and all things science, but every time I walk into this room, my world brightens just a little. There's always something exciting to learn and has my mind whirling with endless possibilities.

If I could do anything with my life, I'd choose to work in one of those fancy labs, studying genetic genealogy. Don't ask me why, but there's something so fascinating about DNA. It draws me in and I find myself getting completely lost in it.

Over the Christmas break last year I'd saved up all my pennies and bought myself a genealogy textbook and was finished with it in days. Between then and now, I think I've read and reread it at least a dozen times.

I drop down into my seat beside Tully and look up at the whiteboard to see which page of our textbooks Mr. Carver wants us looking at today. Eighty-nine. I flip it open and smile down at the textbook.

Looks like we're diving into biochemistry today.

"What are you so happy about?" Tully grunts beside me, pulling out her things before lounging back in her chair.

"Nothing," I say, sliding the textbook towards the top of my desk until Mr. Carver is ready to get started. Though, knowing the kids in this class, he better hurry up or they would have dozed off by the time he even turns around.

"Bullshit," she laughs. "Your eyes lit up like Christmas when you opened the book," she says, reaching for my textbook. "Is there something in here? Did Noah leave you a dirty note?"

"No," I laugh as she scans over the page giving a detailed introduction of Biochemistry. "I just really like this stuff."

Tully's head slowly rotates my way as she gapes at me. "You're shitting me, right?" she questions, double checking the pages for anything that doesn't belong. "This is boring as batshit."

"It is not," I defend. "It's fascinating."

Tully puts a hand to my forehead. "Are you ok? Do you need to see the nurse?"

I swat her away as a chuckle is pulled from my throat. "Shut up," I say, rolling my eyes. "So, I might be a closet nerd."

Her mouth drops open again. "I...I don't even know how to respond to that. You're the queen of not doing your homework and skipping class."

"True, but have you ever seen me walk out of any of my science classes?"

Tully's brows furrow as she thinks it over, not a second later, they fly back up in understanding. "Woah. You're for real, aren't you?" she practically howls with laughter. "You're a science nerd."

"Keep your voice down," I seethe, swatting at her arm and stealing the textbook back. "You're endangering my reputation."

She scoffs. "Like a little nerding out could possibly do that," she laughs. "I could scream it from the rooftop and nobody will believe me. Now, if I said your extracurricular activities included swinging and getting stoned, that they'd believe."

I let out a frustrated sigh. She's probably right. It's a shame though. No one ever expects the popular girls to have brains or even a clue about the world. They all assume that their lives revolve around cell phones, hair, and makeup. Well, guess what? Surprise motherfucker, we're not all plastic bimbos with pea brains.

"I can't even believe this," Tully continues. "How have I never noticed this before?"

"Maybe because you're always too busy plotting revenge tactics in your head or new ways you can piss off Rivers."

A proud grin spreads across her face and lights up her eyes. "I've got some new ones," she tells me. "You want to hear them?"

"Well, duh," I laugh.

"So-"

"Alright, seniors," Mr. Carver's voice rings loudly over our conversation, making Tully's face fall. I mean, from the sparkle in her eyes, she's particularly fond of her new form of torture meant solely for Rivers. Though, the second she has a moment, I don't doubt she'll be telling me all about it. "Time to settle down."

Once we're all quiet enough for Mr. Carver's satisfaction, he gets started on his lesson. "I trust you all have your books open to page eighty-nine?"

I sit up straighter in my chair and face Mr. Carver. He's not the best science teacher I've had over the course of my school years, but he does ok. He's actually interested in his students learning, unlike so many other teachers that teach at Haven Falls Private.

I think the teachers here have already come to the

conclusion that Haven Falls isn't going anywhere. Only a small percentage of students get into college and of those that do, hardly any of them can afford the fees to actually go. It's not ideal. Most of the kids who actually graduate end up working at the grocery store or if they're lucky enough, manage to build up their own business, but honestly, it never goes far as us kids from Haven Falls simply don't have the resources to make it happen.

You'll often find most of the guys fall into careers like landscaping, plumbing or carpentry. All things they can do with their hands while trying to find work in Broken Hill, as they're the only people who can afford to pay straight up.

The girls. They hope they can get themselves pregnant to a guy who has enough money to support her and the baby. Maybe even marry her.

It's a great life here on the wrong side of the tracks.

Like I said, with the students not giving a shit about their futures, why should their teachers? We're lucky to have one like Mr. Carver.

So, my love of science…I don't really think anything will come from it. It's not likely that I'll go to college and it sure as hell isn't likely that I'd be able to afford it. This is it for me. I have to soak up as much of my school years as possible as who the hell knows where I'll be after graduation.

Mr. Carver gets started on his lesson and lets us all know that after a brief introduction into Biochemistry, we'll be heading into the lab to do a little experiment. Excitement surges through me and I will the class to shut up and get on with it.

Nothing's better than actually experimenting.

It's so intriguing. You never know what's going to happen. I mean, well, you always know what *should* happen, but sometimes you get the surprise of your life. It's intoxicating.

As I've already covered the introduction in Biochemistry in my own time with the textbook I bought at Christmas, I find my eyes wandering across the hall to the classroom sitting across from ours. The blinds are pulled halfway down but I can still see the body that sits slouched in a chair, not even slightly interested in what's going on in class.

As if sensing my gaze, Noah's eyes flick across to me. They settle on mine and I find it impossible to look away. He's completely captured me, and I love it.

A playful smile lifts the corner of his lips and fills me with nothing but undeniable joy. My heart rate increases, my breath catches, a smile graces my lips, and I hear nothing except for the rapid pulse beating in my ears. And it's all because of him.

Mr. Carver's voice clears. "Miss Bronx, is there something a little more interesting outside?"

My head whips around to the teacher. Does he want the God's honest truth from me? Because, yeah. There certainly is something a little more interesting outside. I have no doubt that if I was to walk out right now, Noah would follow right along. Tully would probably join out of sheer curiosity until she realized I was leading him somewhere that I could take advantage of him, then she'd scurry away as quickly as possible.

"Uhhhhh," I say, unable to even form a sentence right now. "No."

"Good. Then read out the next paragraph, please."

My eyes zone in on the textbook and I quickly scan page eighty-nine. Shit. Where are we up to?

Tully coughs under her breath beside me. Cough. "Weak Interactions," cough.

I grin into the textbook and pick up at that paragraph as though Tully didn't just save my ass from landing in detention. As I read through the paragraph, I feel Mr. Carver's eyes on me and as I finish and glance up at him, he's giving me a sharp glare through narrowed eyes. "You're lucky you have such good friends, Henley," he says with a clear warning in his tone. "Next time keep your attention on class, not your boyfriend next door."

I nod my head as the rest of the students in the room try their hardest to pretend their queen didn't just get her ass handed to her by the middle-aged science teacher.

As he moves on, picking on Rachel Prairie to read the next section, I can't help but cut my eyes across to Noah once again. His eyes are still on me but that playful smile from before is gone and is replaced with a smugness that makes me want to throat punch him. He saw every moment of me getting in trouble and the bastard absolutely loved it.

I roll my eyes and shake my head, letting him know exactly what I think about that. He brings his fingers to the bottom of his chin and nudges it, silently tell me to keep my chin up before mouthing two simple words that spread warmth all through me. 'Love you.'

I'm sure as hell my eyes are glistening with every damn feeling I have for this guy. 'Love you too,' I mouth right back at him.

He winks and I turn back to Mr. Carver who thankfully is busy reading along with Rachel.

I get focused and do my best not to look across the hall at the boy whose gaze I haven't felt move from me for even a second.

As class goes on, we finally get up and head into the lab for our experiment. I'm the first through the door and the first to pull on my white lab coat and safety glasses. This is my favorite damn part. Nothing beats doing experiments. Except for experimenting with Noah. Though, that's completely unrelated right now.

Tully comes to partner with me then goes to get all the things we'll need while I set up our station.

I partner with Tully nearly every time we have an experiment, but today, she's looking at me with new eyes. She's finally realized that I'm not just in a good mood or wanting to do it quickly to get it over and done with. She's finally realizing that I'm doing it like this because I can't hold myself back.

"Shit," Tully chuckles as she reaches our station and places all the items down. "You really are a little science nerd, aren't you?"

"Uh huh," I murmur, already ignoring her to set up all the items in the order in which we'll need them. "I honestly don't know how you're only just figuring this out now."

"How could I not? I've never seen you do homework before and you're always skipping out on class. I've just never put it together like that. I guess I assumed you were more like me than I had thought."

I smile up at her. "Sorry to disappoint, but I'm not a horny bitch set on revenge."

"You might not be set on revenge," she scoffs, "but you certainly are a horny bitch."

Yeah...I can't deny that. "What can I say?" I shrug. "Your brother brings it out in me."

"Gross," she grunts, scrunching up her face in disgust.

We get busy on our experiment and fall into mindless chatter as we finish setting everything up and measuring chemicals into our beakers. "So, is this what you want to do?" Tully asks, bending low to make sure she's poured the exact amount into her beaker.

I scoff. "In a perfect world, yeah," I tell her. "But you know how it is in Haven Falls. I'll probably end up working as an aide for a chemist...or working at McDonald's."

She rolls her eyes. "With that attitude, you will," she tells me before focusing a glare on me. "And don't knock McDonald's. You'd be privileged to work for such a fine establishment. I mean, those nuggets. Damn. I could eat them all day long."

I can't help but laugh. "Your obsession with chicken nuggets really isn't healthy. You should probably see someone about that."

"And you should probably jump aboard the nugget express before I kick your ass to the curb and tell the world you're a secret loser."

"You wouldn't."

Her green eyes piercing into mine with nothing but seriousness tells me exactly what I need to know. "Wanna bet?"

Shit.

"Fine. I'll leave your ridiculous obsession alone."

"Good. You should have seen what happened to the boys when they tried to give me an intervention. Trust me, that's not a fate I ever want for you."

"Ok, ok," I laugh, holding my hands up in surrender and trying to get back on track. "So, what do you want to do then? After school, I mean."

Tully presses her lips into a tight line and shakes her head vigorously. "Nope. I can't."

"What?" I demand. "Why the hell not? It couldn't be worse than you finding out I want to be a scientist despite the fact that it'll never happen."

"I...nope. I can't."

"Why not?"

"Because you'll laugh at me. I haven't even told my parents about this. Noah and Rivers don't even know. Well, Rivers kind of mentioned it one day but didn't actually realize what he was saying."

I make a cross over my heart. "Promise. I won't laugh."

"No, seriously. It's nothing like you'd expect...like at all."

"Tully," I sigh. "Surely by now, you must realize that if you said you wanted to be a poop technician, I'd support you and figure out how to make it happen."

Her eyes narrow. "Seriously? A poop technician?"

"What?" I laugh. "It couldn't possibly be worse than that."

She quickly glances around but all the other students are way too busy watching their experiments take place to notice what we're talking about. "Alright," she says, slowly. "I want to be a florist." My brows shoot up. "But not just work as a florist, I want my own store and everything."

"Are you serious?"

Her eyes continue flicking around. "Well, yeah."

"That's freaking awesome. Why the hell are you embarrassed about that?"

"Because it's not what people expect me to do with my life. They all think I'm hard. Like I'm supposed to be some kind of badass CEO who gets off by yelling at people all day."

"Don't be stupid," I tell her. "Who gives a shit what other people think? Just because someone else has placed you in their little stereotypical box, doesn't mean that's where you belong. Do what you want to do."

"Yeah, but."

"No. I've never known you to do what others expect of you so why the hell would you do it now? Especially now when it's one of the most important decisions of your life. Who gives a shit what they think?"

"I guess."

"That settles it. You'll have a boutique or floristry or whatever the hell they call them and I'll work there because college is way out of my league."

"Says who?"

"Says every student before me from Haven Falls who's ever tried."

Tully sighs. "Haven Falls does have a really shitty success rate, huh?"

"Sure does," I tell her.

"Girls," Mr. Carver says, striding towards us with purpose, clearly noticing that a little too much chatter has been going on over here. "Tell me about your findings."

Well, two can play at that game. I guess being a bit of a science nerd does have its advantages seeing as though I already know what is supposed to happen during this experiment despite the fact that we haven't got any further than measuring out the chemicals.

I rattle off our 'findings' and half an hour later, we walk back into the classroom feeling as proud as can be.

There are only a few minutes left before the end of class and the end of the school day, so I quickly scrawl out a report in my notebook and wait patiently for the bell to sound.

As I finish a little earlier than expected, I use the last few moments of class to daydream about my hunky boyfriend. I glance up, expecting to find him either staring straight back at me or fast asleep on his desk, but what I don't expect is for him not to be there at all.

I look around what small parts of his classroom I can make out and I'm completely stumped. I pull out my phone and check to see if he's sent me a message. Usually, when he needs to rush out of here to do a shady job for Anton Mathers, he sends me a text. But today, there's nothing.

Damn it.

"Hey," I whisper to Tully. "You didn't get anything from Noah?" I ask. "He's not in class."

Tully looks up and scans his classroom before shrugging her shoulders. "Don't know," she grumbles. "I left my phone in my locker."

Hmmm. How strange.

At least the day is just about over so I can call him as soon as class is done.

The next few minutes are the longest few minutes of my life. I pack up my things and impatiently watch the clock ticking, and as soon as the bell sounds through the classroom, I'm out of my seat in the blink of an eye with Tully right beside me.

We're the first out of the classroom and the first to reach the lockers. We stop by hers first so she can check her phone and when we find nothing, we stop by my locker and grab our things before heading out of the school.

I slip my phone out of the back pocket of my jeans and press Noah's name before bringing the phone up to my ear. Tully rambles on about something as I listen to the call ringing out.

We pass the student office before walking past Principal Evans' office when Tully grabs onto me and howls out in laughter. I turn to see what's caught her attention when I peer through the blinds of Evans' office.

Noah is sitting across from him, elbows pressed on the desk, and an amused smirk on his handsome face telling me that whatever he's being accused of doing right now, he certainly did and he's damn proud of it.

Noah catches us watching him from out the window and grins wide, only making Evans lose his cool, but naturally, Noah doesn't have a single fuck to give.

Geez. I should have known. Of course, he was getting in trouble. If he was on a job, he would have texted because he knows I worry. I hate what he does for Anton and I hate it even more that he won't stop, but it's not my place to ask him too. It's his life and his decision.

Noah feels that he owes Anton for the help he offered his family during the hardest time of their life. There's not a damn thing I can do about it except support him and keep an eye out for him, hoping and praying he doesn't get himself into any trouble.

Seeing us out here, waiting, Noah pushes to his feet, not bothering to allow Evans to finish ranting at him. He makes his way out of the office with Evans yelling behind him, telling him to sit his ass back down, but Noah sees something more important.

Me.

His arm falls over my shoulder as his lips press to my forehead. "Let's go get Ari and go home," he tells me. "I've been missing you."

Well, how could I deny the man what he wants?

"Let's go," I smile before looking back into Evans office to see him scowling at the two of us. "What was going on in there?" I ask. "What did you do?"

His eyes light up with mischief. "Oh nothing," he grins.

"Just a little misunderstanding is all."
   "Bullshit."

CHAPTER 5

I walk through my home with my phone glued to my ear, explaining for the twentieth time what pizza toppings Aria wants. Is it really that hard to understand? It's basically a pepperoni pizza with only a million changes. Maybe we should have gone to the store and gotten all the ingredients. At least that way she can make it herself and have no one to blame when it inevitably comes out wrong.

Dad was supposed to be home two days ago, but the job keeps getting bigger and bigger, then add a flat tire and issues with the brakes, and you've got yourself a job that seriously isn't going as planned.

He checked in with us this morning and I assured him we were doing fine. I can handle it. I think I'm getting better at straddling that fine line between big sister and parent. It's fun but it's also hard work. One thing's for sure though, when it comes time for me to have a kid, I'll be a damn pro.

Just as the guy on the other end of the line gets our order right, my phone buzzes with an incoming text. I peel the phone from my ear and quickly glance at the screen.

Tully – I'm coming over and I'm hungry!!!!!

I press the phone back to my ear with a cringe. "Yeah, I'm going to need to change the order," I tell the guy.

"What?" he panics. "Are you guys throwing some kind of party or something?"

"Sounds about right," I grin, realizing that at some point Noah and Rivers will probably show up and raid the fridge. I add a few pizzas to the list and hang up from my fifteen minute phone call which should have been two or three minutes tops.

I guess that's the price you pay being me.

I drop down on the couch next to Aria and groan, realizing she's finally figured out how to work my Netflix account. She picks some show I've never heard of before and I relax back into the couch.

At least it's a change from *'SpongeBob.'* I don't know how many more episodes I can watch of that show. The theme song has been stuck in my head for weeks. It's driving not only me, but Noah, Rivers, and Tully insane.

I check over Aria's homework to make sure she's on track as we wait for Tully and the pizza guy, and when there's finally a knock at the door, I sigh in relief. I'm so damn hungry and I'm absolutely positive that it's the pizza guy waiting on the other side. Tully would have walked straight in; demanding attention be thrust upon her.

I get up off the couch and grab the cash from the entryway table before pulling open the door. I hear familiar laughter coming from somewhere and see Tully's Jeep behind the pizza delivery guy's shoulder, but don't actually see her.

I make an even trade with the pizza guy and tell him to keep the change before placing the pizza down on the coffee table for Aria to dig into. I remind her that it's hot and let her know that I'll just be outside, searching for Tully.

Aria couldn't care less what I'm doing as long as it doesn't involve blocking her view of the television screen.

I step out front and my eyes follow the sound of Tully's laughter, only for me to gawk at what I see.

Tully is next door, hanging out with Rocko of all people, sitting on the front of his old piece of shit car with the guy standing between her legs. I mean, this is simply taking the whole 'I hate Rivers' thing a little too far.

He murmurs something that I can't quite make out, only for Tully to throw her head back in laughter and playfully smack at his wide chest.

What the fuck is this? Is she blind or stupid? Maybe she doesn't realize who the hell she's talking to. Messing around with Spencer is one thing, but this is just plain stupidity.

Rocko is nothing but bad news, but then, knowing now who Noah and Rivers work for, I guess the same could be said about them. But this is different. Rocko Stevenson isn't a good guy, not like my boys. He's reckless, dangerous, and unpredictable. He's the kind of guy who deserves to be thrown in jail and not just put in a holding cell overnight for trying to jack a car.

Though... that could all just be in my head. I don't actually have any proof of any wrongdoings, it's all just rumors spread through school, but there are too many of them to be ignored.

Tully knows better than to get involved with a guy like him. Noah might forgive me for knowing about Tully and Rivers getting together, but he'll never forgive me if Tully got messed up with the likes of Rocko Stevenson and I didn't try to do anything about it. That would be a game changer for us and I'm not willing to risk what I have with Noah over this stupidity.

I clear my throat, loud enough for the two of them to hear. Tully's head whips around and I expect to see shock or embarrassment at being caught out flirting with the guy, but instead, I get nothing, just a welcoming smile letting me know she's happy to see me. Does she not feel ashamed of herself right now? She should be lunging away from him, not running her fingers over his chest.

"Hey," she calls out. "I'll be there in a sec."

"Actually, could you come now? I kind of need your help with something."

"Oh," she says, looking back at Rocko with an apologetic smile. "I'll see you later," she tells him before leaning into him and pressing a kiss to his cheek as he scowls back at me like a real asshole.

Rocko takes Tully's waist and helps her down from the hood of his car as though she is precious before she hurries over to me. "Hey," she grins, dashing towards my front door as Rocko turns and walks back inside his home. "What's going on? What do you need help with?"

I lead Tully inside and wait until the door is firmly closed behind me before turning on her. "Are you insane?" I demand. "Rocko Fucking Stevenson? Do you have any idea who the hell he is or do you just like flirting with danger?"

Tully glances around as though I've lost my freaking mind. "What are you talking about? There's nothing wrong with Rocko. He just has a bad reputation, just like the rest of us. He's really a nice guy."

"Did you fall and hit your head? Or is this another ploy to get at Rivers because this isn't going to make him jealous, this is going to infuriate him. Not to mention your brother. Are you trying to cause problems between us?"

Tully rolls her eyes and walks past me to sit beside Aria who's turning up the volume on the TV, trying to drown out our conversation. "Don't you think you're being a little dramatic?" she says as I snatch the television remote from Aria and put the volume back to a normal level which doesn't threaten to burst my eardrums.

"Dramatic?" I shriek. "You've got to be kidding."

"I'm not. Serious. Rocky is actually really nice. He's fun and flirty and despite what you might think of him, I actually kind of like him. He's the only guy who's managed to get my mind off Rivers even if it's only for a second."

I groan and let my head fall to the back of the couch. "No," I almost cry. "Don't tell me that."

"Sorry," she grunts, "but it's true."

"So, it's not just a ploy to piss off Rivers?"

"No," she laughs. "That's just an added bonus."

I let out a heavy breath. "You really like him?"

"Well," she says, deep in thought. "I think so. I mean, if he asks me out, I'm not going to say no."

"Damn it," I groan. "Any guy would be stupid not to ask you out."

"Yeah," she laughs. "I like to think so too."

"This isn't the first time you've spent time with him, is it?"

Guilt flashes through her green eyes as she glances up from the pizza selections before her. "No," she admits. "I came over here on Friday night not realizing you'd gone to Noah's race and he was out front working on his car and we got talking. He gave me his number and we've been texting ever since."

Hurt flares through me. "That was five days ago," I tell her. "Why the hell haven't you said anything?"

Tully scoffs as she takes a huge bite of pizza and then tries to talk around it. "So I could avoid this interrogation," she tells me. "You're just like Noah and Rivers. Act first, ask questions later."

"I did do that, didn't I?"

She swallows the pizza. "Uh huh."

"Sorry," I cringe.

"Don't be sorry for being who you are. I've known that about you since day one and I decided to love you anyway."

"Yeah, well, that's your fault then," I grumble before looking up at her. "You know, no matter who you date or who's trying to get in your pants, you and Rivers will always belong together. No one else will ever measure up to what you two have."

Tully sighs deeply as a sadness seeps into her. "Don't

remind me," she murmurs. "But it's not like I can magically force him to be with him. He doesn't want me, no matter what I do. I told him, right to his face that I'm crazy in love with him and it's still not enough. I'll never be enough for him, so I have no choice but to try and move on."

"Don't put this on you," I tell her, absolutely furious with her. "You are more than enough. He's just as in love with you as you are with him and you know it. He just has some twisted issues that he needs to sort out, and one day, we're going to figure out what they are and help him through it, but until then, you need to be patient. He'll come back to you when he's ready."

"But it might be too late by then."

"That's just the risk he has to take. I don't expect you to just forget about him and move on, but just don't completely close yourself off to him either. He'll eventually come around and I'd hate to think that when that does happen, that you're not willing to let yourself find your happiness."

"Stop," she says, getting watery eyes. "You're making me get all emotional."

"Sorry," I grumble. "I just want you to be happy like I am and I know that Rivers has been an ass, but I still believe you guys will find a way to make it work."

"I'm not so sure," she tells me. "I think it's run its course."

I let out a sigh, hating that she's hurting so much right now. Maybe I should just let her explore her options with Rocko. After all, she knows all the rumors just as I do, yet out of the both of us, she's the only one who had a proper conversation with the guy. Maybe I do have him wrong. Maybe he is an alright guy.

Either way, I have a feeling we're about to find out.

I reach for a pizza as the door practically flies off its hinges before two huge guys barge their way through the living room as though they own the place. Noah slams the door shut behind them before inhaling the heavenly aroma of pizza on the coffee table and fist pumping the sky. "Yes," he cheers, looking right into my soul. "It's like you read my fucking mind."

I roll my eyes as Rivers practically barges his way past me and drop downs in front of Tully. "What's wrong?" he demands, taking in her watery eyes and making Noah more alert than ever.

Tully brings up her foot and places it on Rivers' shoulder before pushing him away from her. "Nothing," she grumbles, glancing away and refusing to meet his eyes. "Just choked on my food is all."

Rivers narrows his eyes on her for a moment before glancing to me, hoping he'll find some answers within my eyes, but not today. I'm a closed book and in this situation, I'm with Tully. I know they're both hurting over this, but Tully is the one who needs me more.

Noah cuts the tension in the room as he storms in front of me and scoops up a slice of pizza before taking another. He puts one upside down, on top of the other like a pizza sandwich before hoisting me up off the couch. He takes my seat, dropping down beside his sister with me on his lap and takes the biggest bite of pizza I've ever seen. I mean, how was that even possible?

I lean into his chest and he curls his arm around me. "How was your night?" I ask with sarcasm. "Did you enjoy being a drug mule or were you kept busy stealing a car?"

"Neither," he grins. "Collecting a debt."

Tully scoffs. "Is that why Rivers' knuckles are bloodied?"

Noah shrugs his shoulders. "The guy wouldn't pay up and I don't want to be the sorry bastard who has to go back and tell Anton that we didn't come through."

"And did you, come through, I mean?"

"Don't I always come through?" he murmurs before pressing his lips to my neck.

I can't help but smile as a moan slips from my lips. "Yeah, you do."

"Damn straight, Spitfire."

Tully leans forward and takes a sip of her soda as her eyes worriedly rake over Rivers' hand once again, hating seeing him in any sort of pain. She looks to her brother. "So, how come he had to be the one to do the damage? What's wrong with fucking up your knuckles?"

Rivers scoffs as a smile crosses his lips but it's Noah who speaks up. "Because I lost the fucking bet."

"Wait, what? You make that sound like a bad thing," I say.

"Come on, Spitfire," Noah grins. "Don't act like you don't know how good it feels to nail some dickhead in the jaw."

Tully nods her head, completely in agreement with her brother while I let out a sigh. "Yeah, ok. You've made your point."

"Good," he says, pulling me in a little tighter. "Now, what have you guys been doing all afternoon?"

Tully's eyes flare open as I quickly cover for the two of us. I mean, they really don't need to know what we've just spent the afternoon discussing. "Nothing," I tell him. "Just chilling."

"No," Aria yells out, flying to her feet and staring angrily at me as she looks away from the TV for the first time in over an hour. "Don't lie. That was a lie."

"What?" I demand with wide eyes as Noah's hand flinches on my waist.

"What's she talking about?"

"Nothing," I say.

"No," Aria demands, stomping her little foot on the ground. "You were fighting with Tully. You yelled at her."

Noah grumbles beside me, sitting up a little straighter to see Aria better as Rivers just looks on in confusion. "What are you talking about, Ari?"

Aria looks at Noah. "Henley was yelling at Tully and told her she can't play with the boy next door."

Shit.

"Rocko?" Rivers grunts.

Aria nods her little head as Tully's world comes crumbling down. I reach out and squeeze her hand. "Sorry," I tell her. "I tried."

"I know," she sighs. "I know."

Not a second later, all hell breaks loose.

CHAPTER 6

The wind whips through my hair as I stand by the side of the track watching Noah speed across the finish line like a damn boss. He slams on the brakes and his white Camaro skids to a stop, spitting up a cloud of dust behind him. I swear, it's one of the hottest things I've ever seen.

I don't know how he does it but there's something about Noah Cage behind the wheel of a car that gets me each and every time. I mean, damn. Maybe it's the cocky, too sure confidence paired with the mischievous green, sparkling eyes that drive me crazy. Add the bad boy vibe and sexy as hell tatts and I'm a freaking goner.

I watch in amusement as he pulls himself up through the open window of his Camaro and perches himself there to show off to his adoring fans as though he's some kind of A-list celebrity.

He cheers and they cheer right along with him making both me and Tully shake our heads. Tully's head shake is more from mere embarrassment whereas mine is out of exasperation. The beaming smile on my face though, that's not going anywhere.

Noah turns to start searching me out and it only takes a second. It's as though there's some kind of magnetic force between us that draws us together. He always seems to be able to find me in a crowd and I absolutely love that about him, except for those few times I don't. Tully and I have a habit of trying to slip away at parties to enjoy ourselves without Noah looming over us, making sure we're always protected and safe. Rivers can be worse though. Like damn, is it too much to ask for us girls to be able to let loose and have a bit of wild fun?

With my eyes locked firmly on his, Noah raises his chin as if to remind me that he's the fucking boss around here. Though, maybe I should tell him that I saw Nate Ryder hanging out over by the Broken Hill side not long ago. If Noah is a boss around here, that must make Nate the King, right? He holds all the records and while he's been away working and going to college, Noah has been quickly taking over. I guess they're both kings in their own right.

Seeing the next race starting to set up, Noah and his opponent get back into their cars and practically barge the crowd off the track. I watch as he drives his Camaro back up to where the rest of the cars are parked and brings it to a stop. He grabs his hoodie then mine, and finally rushes his ass back over to me.

"Here," he says, throwing my hoodie at me before I get a chance to tell him how great he was. "It's getting cold. I don't want you getting sick and putting your dirty ass germs all over me."

"You're so charming," I grin, pulling the hoodie over my head before releasing my hair out the back.

"You know it," he says, putting his arm over my shoulder and pulling me into his side as he looks down at the race that's about to start. "Where's Rivers?"

I shrug my shoulders as Tully grunts out, "Over there."

I look across at her and then follow her heavy scowl to

our right where Rivers stands amongst a few of the other seniors from school. That usually wouldn't pull any sort of reaction out of her, but the way some random chick keeps hanging off him despite the way he keeps pushing her off is enough to drive Tully insane.

"Fucking girls," Noah scoffs beside me, shaking his head at the pure desperation written all over the skank. He looks around me to Tully. "What are you so pissed about? Aren't you over your little crush on him yet?"

Tully turns on her brother and the look in her eyes is enough to have even the strongest of men squirming, but not Noah, he just grins back at his twin sister as though he just asked her what color the sky is. He should be worried though. I'm honestly fearing for the safety of his pretty face right now. "You're a real asshole, you know that," she seethes before storming away.

"Shit," Noah laughs. "What's her fucking problem?"

"You don't want to know," I grumble, silently hoping he doesn't ask me more on the topic.

He watches as she walks away and I cringe as she heads straight for Rocko's arms. Shit. This isn't going to be good.

Noah stiffens beside me and I watch from the corner of my eye as Rivers readjusts his position in his group to get a better view of her. The boys seriously don't like this just the same as me, but there's not a lot we can do about it. She's a big girl and we have to let her make her own decisions and if we don't, there will be hell to pay.

Noah goes to take a step and I latch onto him a little tighter. "Don't," I beg. "Just…give her tonight. You can rant at her when we get home. If you get all pissy on her now, you're just going to embarrass her and then she'll get payback by practically throwing herself at him."

"Damn it," he growls, knowing I'm right. "I don't like it."

"I know," I tell him. "Neither do I, but she insists that he's not as bad as we think, and we need to give her space to explore that."

"But he's going to hurt her."

"Tully's tough. If anything, she'll be the one doing the hurting."

Noah lets out a frustrated groan before pulling his eyes away from his twin sister. "She'll be alright," I tell him. "And besides, it's not like Rivers is going to take his eyes off her for even a second. She's safe."

"She's like a sitting duck over there," he murmurs.

"You can't think of her as a fragile little girl. That's not who she is anymore. She's a lot stronger than you give her credit for," I tell him, weaving my fingers through his and giving them a squeeze. "Now, leave her the hell alone before she comes back over here and punches you in the ovaries."

He looks down at me, wondering if I just called him a girl or if I'm seriously confused about the male and female sexes. "Why the hell would she do that? I didn't do anything wrong."

"Believe me, she could find something to blame on you."

"You fucking girls," he says, shaking his head. "You know, sometimes I just don't get you."

"Good," I chuckle, looking up at him. "Then it's working."

"What's working?"

"You'll never know."

His eyes sparkle but the next race starts and completely steals his attention, giving me a moment to melt into his side and just enjoy being in his arms. We very rarely get a chance to just be us. Living in Haven Falls, there's always someone around. It's either Rivers or Tully and if it's not them, then it's the parents or Aria. When we finally escape them, we get hit with the phone calls and text messages of all the people from school wanting attention, and once that's finally sorted, Anton will drag his ass away.

Not now, though. This is our time and I'm not going to waste a single second of it. Rivers and Tully both seem busy, all the kids from school have already pined over his attention, and apparently, Anton is away on 'business' for the night, meaning I have Noah all to myself.

"Why don't we get out of here?" I ask as my eyes follow the cars drifting around the track.

"We will," he promises. "I just want to see something first."

"Like what?"

"You'll see," he says, grinning down at me. "Have you seen Kaylah yet? Do you want to say 'hey' real quick?"

My eyes shoot across to where the Broken Hill kids hang out. "Oh, is she here?" I ask. "I haven't seen her."

"Yeah, I saw Jesse's Range Rover earlier. I'm assuming she's with him."

"Probably," I laugh. I mean, wherever Jesse goes, Kaylah's not far behind. Those two are like stuck like glue. They're madly in love to the point it's nearly sickening. I wonder if that's what me and Noah look like to the rest of the world.

Noah starts leading me around the track and it's not long before we have all the kids from Broken Hill scowling at us, wondering why the fuck we dared to wander over to their side of the track. The scowls instantly stop as Kaylah turns around and gives us a welcoming smile.

"Hey," she smiles widely before pulling me into a tight hug. "I wondered if you were here. I saw Noah's race."

At the mention of his name I glance up to find him saying 'hey' to all the guys of this group, though apart from Jesse, Nate, and Jackson, I can't actually remember any of them.

"Yeah," I tell her as I watch Noah give an awkward nod to Jackson that makes me want to howl with laughter. That certainly wasn't the same welcoming backslap that he gave the other guys, but I can't blame him, he's not exactly a massive fan of Jackson's. "If I knew you were here, I would have found you earlier."

"Don't worry about it," she says. "I sent you a text when Noah was racing but I assumed you were a little preoccupied."

My hands instinctively feel my ass for my phone. "Shit, I think my phone's in Noah's car."

"Eh," she shrugs. "You're here now." With that, she pulls me into her group and practically throws me at Tora. After she helped me take down Monica a few weeks ago, Kaylah has been desperately trying to get me and Tora to become besties, but as much as I like the girl, I'm not one for having a million friends. I have Tully and Kaylah and they're more than enough for me to keep up with.

I say 'hi' to the other girls whose names I've completely forgotten as the last time we met; I was probably under the influence of who the hell knows what. Jackson comes forward and gives me a big hug and I watch as Noah stiffens.

Jackson hurt me in a way that I'll never be able to forget, and Noah absolutely hates that despite the fact that I've managed to forgive him. He took my virginity when he should have sent me home. It wasn't special and it wasn't how I wanted my first time to be, but it is what it is. One day I'll be able to look at Jackson and see the friend I grew up with, but until then, he'll continue being the guy who took advantage of a love-sick teenage girl.

There's so much history there I doubt I'll hold onto the pain much longer. Especially now that I have Noah. He makes me forget all the bad things. I hardly think about mom anymore, I don't dwell on the fact that Jackson and Kaylah took off and left me with nothing, and I don't hate on the bitches who made my life hell at school.

Maybe I've done some growing up over the past few months, or maybe being with Noah has just opened my eyes to what's really important.

All I know is that I don't want it to change. I'm in a happy place right now and I've never felt so strong. To lose this would be a tragedy.

Noah practically takes my hand and rips me away from Jackson despite the fact that my feelings for him died a long time ago, but what can I say, I knew he was a possessive asshole when we first met, and to be honest, it's kind of hot. We say goodbye to the Broken Hill crew and I promise Kaylah that I'll ditch Noah and hang out with her tomorrow.

With all the eyes of the Broken Hill students still on us, we duck back over to our side of the track where we can continue being the rock stars that we are rather than the scum that the other side sees us as.

By the time we get back to where we were before, a new race is starting to take place and I look down at the track to see a very familiar black Charger. Pulling up next to a black Camaro. "Is that Nate and Jackson racing?" I ask with a gasp, having Déjà vu. After all, the last time I saw these two cars racing, one of them ended upside down and off the side of the track. I continue trying to make out the people in the cars and realize each car has a passenger too. "Wait. Are Tora and Elle racing with them?"

"Yep," Noah says with a grin.

Shit. Those girls have balls to race with those idiots. I guess that's even more of my respect those two have just earned themselves, and I have to admit, Tora's doing pretty damn well for herself in my book. "Should they be doing this?" I ask Noah. "The last race didn't end so well and I only just started liking them."

Noah laughs. "I think Nate and Jackson are on good terms now," he says. "It should be a clean race, but every fucker and his dog are going to be talking about this for years to come."

I look up at the strange tone in his voice. "Why's that?"

"You'll see."

Noah turns back to the two black cars down on the track as my attention falls towards Rivers. He's still watching Tully but it's almost as though he wants to watch the race too. Kind of amusing actually.

A hush falls over the crowd on either side of the track and it doesn't take a genius to realize that the race of the century is about to start. My eyes snap down to the track to find a girl in a black string bikini walk between the Camaro and Charger and all I can think is that she must be cold. I mean, it's deathly freezing out here tonight. If Noah was worried about me getting sick, then it would only make sense for him to be petrified for her.

The engines roar and the guys haven't even taken off yet. Noah's hand tightens around mine and not a second later, the bikini wearing girl drops her handkerchief, starting the most anticipated race this track has ever seen.

Dust flies up behind them as they each take off like bats out of hell. I can just imagine the girls in the passengers' seats. Elle is probably shitting herself while Tora would be egging Nate on to go faster. Me? I'd probably be trying to straddle Noah while he tried to push me off.

I wonder if it could work? Hmm, maybe we should test that theory.

Mind meet gutter.

The crowd is dead silent, the only noise I hear is their audible gasps when the cars hit the first corner. Nate instantly takes the lead.

Their cars are deafening as they race around the track and it seems like every second is drawn out as though I'm watching it in slow motion, but at the same time, if I was to blink, I'd miss it. "This is nuts," I tell Noah, so damn pleased he doesn't have some ridiculous rivalry with the Broken Hill guys.

"Uh huh," he agrees.

Nate gets a whole car length in front of Jackson and I feel a slight pang rip through me. I'm so used to rooting for Jackson that the thought of him being behind right now sits kind of funny within me.

They hit a bend and Nate sails around it effortlessly just moments before Jackson hurries around behind him which is when he speeds the hell up or Nate ridiculously finds his brake as somehow, they're now side by side. "Oh, shit,"

Noah chuckles beside me, sounding way too happy about this.

"What?"

"Nate's playing with him."

"Huh? What the hell are you talking about?"

Noah watches eagerly. "He's letting Jackson think he has a shot," he laughs. "You watch, as soon as they hit the final straight, he'll smoke him."

"How the hell do you know that?"

A grin lifts the corner of his lips. "Because I would have done the exact same thing."

I roll my eyes and despite the fact that Noah thinks we already have a clear winner, I still can't look away.

A screeching noise sounds behind us before red and blue flashing lights light up the darkened track. "Fuck," Noah yells, holding onto my hand a little tighter. It takes me a moment to catch up with what the fuck is going on, but after gaping at the cop cars behind me, I quickly realize the place is being raided. "We have to go. NOW."

Shit hits the fan.

Kids start running for cars, people crash into one another, and cops try to round people up like a heard of sheep. But they should know better. It's every man for themselves. It's nothing but fucking chaos.

Noah holds onto me a little tighter, terrified of losing me in this crowd. If I go down, that's where I'll stay as I can guarantee that nobody is sparing a second to save me from getting trampled.

Panic seeps into me and I quickly start looking around. "Where's Tully?" I yell over the chaos, distantly noticing that Nate and Jackson haven't let up on their race. They should be leaving. What the fuck are they doing?

Noah pauses a second and a tightness appears in his back as he searches for his sister. "There," he yells back over his shoulder. I follow his gaze and let out a sigh as I see her. She's all but stumbling behind Rivers, desperately trying to keep up with his long strides as he clutches her hand in his.

Knowing she's safe, Noah makes a break for it.

We bolt for his Camaro, pleased to see that the cops seem to be heading for Nate and Jackson seeing as though in this situation, they're the only ones being caught red-handed. Thank God Noah's race was already over and done with. Though, I guess it sucks to be Nate and Jackson. They're on their own now.

I struggle to keep up with Noah as he hauls me through the mess of bodies. People crash into me and I don't doubt that I'll be covered in bruises afterward.

A girl's high-pitched scream rips past my ear and my head whips around, searching out the noise. I see her almost instantly. A small brunette girl fumbles to the ground, her body being jostled around in every direction.

"Shit," I screech, pulling back on Noah's hand, desperate to help the girl as if I don't, she's not going to come out of this very well.

"Come on," Noah says, tugging back on my hand.

I squeeze my fingers free of his tight grasp and double back for her. People smack into me on their way past as I head in the opposite direction of the crowd. Handbags and elbows connect against me, but determination gets the better of me.

By the time I reach the girl, she's curled up on the ground with her arms protectively hovering over her head. I reach for her, but she's too terrified, she can't even feel me pulling on her arm. Something crashes into my back and I stumble forward, only able to keep on my feet as Noah grabs me with his strong hands and steadies me before I make this situation so much worse.

"Help me," I beg him, still clawing at the girl's arm, trying to pull her up.

Noah glances back towards his car with a cringe before looking down at the girl. In one easy swoop, he bends down and grabs her. Not a second later, she's over his shoulder, his hand firmly clutching mine, and we're running as fast as we can towards his Camaro.

We reach his car in less than thirty seconds. Tully and Rivers are already here, waiting desperately for Noah to hurry up and unlock the car.

Noah practically hurls the girl at Rivers before diving in the driver's seat. The rest of us pile in and within the blink of an eye, Noah is racing down the dirt road that leads out of here, overtaking the rest of the idiots with practiced ease until he's breaking out onto the highway.

"Fuck," he breathes as cops spill out behind us.

I turn in my seat, eyes quickly flashing through the back window. There are at least four cops behind us, but there's a shitload of kids from the races for them to go after.

If Noah plays this smart, we'll get out of here in no time.

Noah kicks it up a notch and speeds through the traffic without blinking an eye. I've said it before and I'll say it again, there's no doubt in my mind that Noah could be a professional racer. He's just that good. The cops don't even bother heading our way. There are easier targets on this road right now.

A scream comes from the backseat and I whip my head around to watch the random girl sitting between Rivers and Tully getting thrown from side to side, clearly terrified of the speed at which Noah is handling his car. Rivers latches onto her, trying to steady her, but it's no use. There's not really much for her to hold onto in the middle.

Rivers grabs her seatbelt and overcrowds her personal space as he buckles her in, though it's not long before Noah completely loses the cops and is able to slow down.

"Holy shit," she gasps. "That was insane."

Rivers grins down at her, clearly pleased that she thinks so, but Noah has a different idea. "Who are you?" Noah demands, glancing up at her in his rearview mirror and not sparing a moment to appease her. After all, he doesn't like people coming in on his pack and right now, she's sitting right in the middle of it, getting front row tickets to our lives.

Her eyes widen a fraction, having to readjust her thoughts on the guy who just saved her ass. "I'm Alyssa. I'm new. I just transferred to Haven Falls," she explains, "My first day is on Monday."

Noah grunts as Tully scoffs. "You've fallen in with the wrong people if you're already at the races."

"Yeah, I think I'm working that out," she murmurs, letting out a deep breath before sucking in another, trying to calm herself.

"It's alright, babe," Rivers says softly. "You can chill with us."

"Babe?" Tully shrieks at Rivers, across the new girl who sits as still as possible, terrified of even making a peep. "You met the girl ten seconds ago and you're calling her 'babe'?

Oh no. This isn't going to be good.

"What's it to you?" Rivers shoots right back at her. "I wonder what you were calling Rocko tonight? Oh, and it was nice of him to get you the fuck out of there instead of leaving you to fend for yourself by the way. Such a fucking gentleman."

Tully launches herself across the backseat with a battle cry as Alyssa desperately tries to unbuckle herself. "Feel free to drop me off at any time," she calls into the front while Rivers tries to save his face from being clawed.

"You're a fucking bastard, Rivers," Tully yells as Noah and I watch on from the front seat, not at all fazed by the little catfight going on in the back.

"Where am I taking you, Alyssa?" Noah questions, not one to like the random girl intruding.

She scoffs under her breath, still trying to get away from the flailing arms and legs. "Anywhere is good."

"Alright," Noah shrugs before pulling off to the side of the road.

"Don't be a fucking bastard," Rivers scolds. "Take the girl home. Don't leave her on the side of the road. Anything could happen to her out here and you don't want that on your conscience."

Noah groans and ten minutes later, we're pulling up at the girl's house with Tully practically held down on Rivers lap, his arms wrapped around her like steel vices, refusing to let her release the Kraken again.

I guess tonight's fun is far from over.

CHAPTER 7

I step through the threshold of the cafeteria on Monday afternoon and let out a deep sigh. I can't believe it's only lunchtime. Today seems to be dragging on like you wouldn't believe.

It was a shitty weekend to follow up the shitty Friday night at the races. Well, maybe that isn't completely fair. Friday was a pretty awesome night before the shit hit the fan.

Tully and Rivers have been at each other's throats all weekend and it's getting a little too much to bear. Maybe we all need a trip away or something to help us find the love again because the way things are with them right now, it's really starting to grate on my nerves. I doubt it will be long before Noah puts two and two together. Right now, he just thinks they're being their usual idiotic selves. If only he knew.

My eyes scan the cafeteria and I quirk a brow seeing Alyssa sitting right beside Rivers at our table with his arm over her shoulder. Noah's eyes meet mine across the room and I can practically hear his scoff from here followed by a look that tells me not to even ask.

But where's Tully?

I continue scanning the room as I stride towards Noah.

Ahhh, she's over by the football team, sitting on the table as they all drool at her feet. I should have known.

This shit is getting out of hand.

I drop down beside Noah and meet Tully's eyes, letting her know that I'm here and it's safe to come back in case she needs a buffer. Either that or we can gang up on Alyssa and teach her the hard way to stay away from what Tully has already claimed as her own.

No. That's maybe pushing the friendship with Rivers.

I steal the bright red, juicy looking apple from in front of Noah and take a bite before he has a chance to rescue it from my clutches. Mmmm, yeah. Just as good as I had imagined.

I lean into Noah and people watch as the world goes by around us. Tully ignores us as best as she can as I do my best to tune out the secretive murmurs coming from Rivers and Alyssa. This isn't going to be good. Hopefully, we can get through lunch without Tully making some sort of scene, but don't be fooled, the second school is out and we're sheltered with privacy, shit's going to hit the fan.

I almost feel sorry for Alyssa. She's new. She couldn't possibly understand what she's just gotten herself involved in, or well, what Rivers has dragged her into. And on her first day too. Sucks to be her.

I doubt Rivers even likes her. Don't get me wrong, she's pretty and I'm sure he's going to screw her anyway or at least tell Tully that he did. I can just see it now. Tully is going to go nuts with jealousy and the rage will eventually take over. She'll tear the poor girl apart and Rivers will come out looking like the innocent one.

Yeah, it really, really sucks to be Alyssa.

I should have left her on the ground to be trampled by the masses. That would have probably been a better outcome for her as the wrath of Tully Cage is a scary thing.

I take another bite of Noah's apple before resting my

head down on the cool table. Aria had me up early again this morning, despite the fact that dad got home yesterday. It was supposed to be my sleep in day, but I guess that was wishful thinking when you live with a five year old.

My only saving grace is that dad's picking Aria up this afternoon so I can head straight to Noah's place and hopefully have a relaxing night with my boyfriend. You know, that's if Tully can entertain herself for a while and not need me to rant at. Considering what's happening right now, I have a feeling I'll be witnessing a little more than ranting tonight.

I close my eyes, loving the serenity the darkness brings with it. Now if only I could somehow block out the noise, and transport myself to my bed, it would be absolutely perfect. Noah's hand runs up and down my back. "You alright, Spitfire?"

"Mmm," I sigh. "Just tired."

"K," he murmurs as his hand trails up from my back and starts playing in my hair, just about sending me off to sleep. "Do you want to get out of here?"

"Can't," I tell him. "I've got an exam after lunch."

He mumbles something that's barely audible and when he doesn't prompt me for some kind of reply, I let it go. I hear someone drop down on the table in front of us and I do my best to tune that out too. A low voice sounds and strikes up a conversation with Noah and after his third sentence, I recognize the voice belonging to Jared Frazer, one of the seniors who actually isn't too bad to hang out with.

Noah talks with him a while as I continue eating his apple and resting my head on the table. I can't help but let out a relaxed sigh. This is nice. For once nobody is screaming for my attention, there's no one currently trying to tear me down, and there are no skanky cheerleaders trying to convince my boyfriend that he's her baby daddy. Like I said, it's freaking nice.

I could get used to this, only I know it's not going to last.

Hell, I doubt I'll even get to the end of the day before some kind of drama stirs up. That's just the way of life, right?

I finish off the apple and push myself to my feet with a low guttural groan before slowly making my way across the cafeteria to the trash can. I dump the apple core in and quickly do another search for Tully.

Yep. She's still more than happily occupied by the football team.

I turn back to Noah with sleepy eyes and start making my way back to him. Maybe I should have taken his offer and gotten out of here. I'm so damn tired. I'm probably going to fall asleep during my exam.

A too loud voice cackles right by my ear and I jerk around, completely taken surprise by the guy suddenly standing two feet behind me. "When are you going to share the love, babe?" says Jack Saunders, another senior, who, unfortunately, is not as cool to hang out with as Jared Frazer.

"What?" I grunt out, extremely unladylike as I feel Noah's eyes piercing into my back.

Jack grins. "You've been giving it up for Spence, right? Everyone's talking about it."

I didn't just hear that, did I? Maybe he's confused. Got the wrong girl, perhaps.

"Wait. What?" I say, scrunching my face up in confusion as I notice how tight his body is. Though this isn't something new. Guys tend to be nervous around me. Either scared of me or terrified of what Noah would do to them if they talk to me. "Who's giving it up for Spencer?"

Jack steps a little closer, pulling out his cocky attitude. "Rumor has it, you are. He said you fucked him out back of some party a few weeks ago." His grin widens. "He said you were fucking wild. So, I'm just wondering, is this some kind of deal you've got going with him and Noah? You fuck them both whenever they're down?"

Oh, this guy is about to need a facial reconstruction. I hope he has his Mumma's plastic surgeon on speed dial.

"You know who you're talking to, right?" I question, in case he's a little dumb. Where the hell did this information come from anyway? I fooled around with Spencer once and while he was great with his tongue, I couldn't go through with it because he isn't my bad boy covered in tattoos. I certainly didn't screw him and it's certainly not some ongoing arrangement.

Jack looks down at me as though I'm trash and the disgust in his eyes in nearly enough to paralyze me. "Yeah, baby. I know exactly who I'm talking to. You gave it up for Jackson, then Noah, and now Spence," he winks as he licks his lips. "About time you sat on my cock and went for a ride, don't ya think?" His eyes trail over my body. "Besides, you'd be fun. With all that experience under your belt, a girl like you would have a few party tricks."

Oh dear. The poor guy. He just signed his death certificate.

A breathy laugh escapes me, and I know I'm going to have to move quickly before Noah gets over here to put the trash out.

I bite my lip as though I'm actually turned on by this fucker and give him my best bedroom eyes. His body responds instantly. His eyes become hooded and the guarded tension in his body leaves, feeling he actually has some kind of shot, probably unable to believe his luck.

I step into him, taking hold of his belt buckle as I look up at him. "Is that what you like?" I whisper. "A woman who knows what she's doing? Someone who could rock your fucking world and leave in the morning without a goodbye?"

His hand curls around my waist and I can practically feel the fury rolling off Noah behind me, but it's clear he's giving me space to handle this myself. "Well, that's what you do for Noah and Spencer, right?" Jack murmurs. "Why not add another name to your list? I'll make it worth your while."

Wait. Is he calling me a prostitute right now?

I pull on his belt buckle, bringing his hips forward. "Well

see," I wink. "If you play your cards right, I might just play you right back." I watch him swallow and then follow my movements as I run my tongue over my lip. I indicate for him to duck down so I can whisper in his ear. "Tell me, Jack," I murmur. "How do you like it? I bet you're rough, aren't you?"

He breathes out a laugh, unable to believe his fucking luck. "Yeah, I do."

BAM.

I nail the fucker in the gut with one hell of an uppercut and I don't dare hold back. Jack doubles over, groaning as he clutches his stomach. "Is that how rough you like it?" I demand, grabbing his shoulders and slamming my knee up into his groin.

"Fuck, stop," he moans, falling to the ground at my feet.

I stand over him like a fucking boss. "Maybe next time you'll remember who the fuck you're talking to," I announce loud enough for the people around us to hear, letting it act as a reminder for the rest of the fucktards around here that they can't mess with me. Not now and especially not when I'm tired as fuck.

Noah's at my side with Rivers, and Tully in the blink of an eye. "What the fuck was that about?" Noah demands, looking down at Jack holding onto his junk as though it's about to detach from his body and shrivel up to die.

My hand slides into Noah's, needing his touch to calm me down and stop me from going apeshit on this douche. "Spencer's been telling everyone that I'm fucking him and Jack here thought he could get in on the action."

Noah's head whips around to me. "Excuse me?"

"That's right. You heard me, big guy."

Rivers grunts under his breath. "Fuck."

In the blink of an eye, Noah has Jack by the scruff of his shirt and is holding him up, his feet dangling below him as he desperately tries to squirm free but it's no use, Noah's steel grip and strength are unbreakable. "Where the fuck do you get off talking to my girl?"

Jack's eyes go wide as the rest of the cafeteria looks on, waiting to see their king put a mere peasant in his place. "I fucking asked you a question," Noah roars loud enough to draw the attention of the whole faculty. Hell, probably loud enough for the fuckers in Broken Hill to know shit's about to go down.

"I...I...I'm sorry, man," he stutters out. "It was a joke. We were just having a little fun."

"Insinuating my girlfriend is a whore and asking her to fuck you is your idea of fun?" Noah questions.

Jack's eyes flick around the cafeteria, silently begging his peers for help but not a damn finger comes to his aide. The douchebag dug his grave and now it's time to lay in it. "I'm sorry," he repeats before glancing at me. "Fuck, Henley. I'm sorry, alright? It was a joke."

I step into him. "A joke, hey?" I question. "You've got a little sister, right? Liza. A sophomore? Maybe Rivers should go and play a little joke on her. See how she likes big fuckers coming and harassing her during lunch. Maybe he'll step in nice and close and let her know she's a dirty little slut. Maybe he'll touch her just enough to draw her in before demanding she drop down on his cock and bounce around like a little bunny. Tell me, does it sound like such a funny joke now? Because it sounds fucking hilarious to me."

The thought has Aria popping into my head and all I can think about is that shit like this shouldn't fly anymore. She's only little and rumors around here spread like wildfire. I can't have her hearing this kind of shit about me. It would destroy her. She wouldn't understand what was going on and that would hurt more than I could possibly know.

Jack panics, though if he knew anything about us, he'd know that we would never stoop so low as to follow through on a threat like that. Noah and Tully had Lily and I have Aria. This is the very last thing any of us would want, we're protective of little sisters. In our eyes, they're precious, but

76

this dickhead doesn't need to know that. "Fuck. No. Leave Liza out of this."

Noah grows tired of my taunting and tightens his hold on Jack. "When was Spencer running his mouth?"

Jack's eyes flick from me and back to Noah before looking over Rivers, probably making sure he's staying still for the time being. "He…he was running his mouth this morning."

Noah practically growls. This could have easily been Jack putting stories together from all the rumors going around about me. I mean, after fooling around with Spencer all those weeks ago, a few whispers were spread, and naturally, the whole school knew about Jackson. But for this to be a new rumor from Spencer himself, that means game on.

Our fight isn't with Jack. It's with Spencer and he's about to get the shock of his life.

Hmm, maybe now's a good time for Tully to come clean about sleeping with him a few weeks ago. Though, timing is everything and that might just push Noah to do something that will see him behind bars for the rest of his life.

Just because I think he's hands down incredible, doesn't exactly mean he's a saint. Noah would definitely take it too far if his head wasn't in the right space and that scares the crap out of me. I don't want to be visiting my boyfriend in jail for the rest of my life. Just thinking about all the missed spontaneous, steamy nights together terrifies me. That would definitely be a tragedy.

I turn to Noah. "Put out the trash."

A devilish grin lifts the corner of his lips and he's more than happy to comply. Noah takes one step and with an incredible show of strength, launches Jack a few feet across the room until he crashes down into the nearly overflowing trash can.

The cafeteria bursts into a flurry of activity. Kids from every corner start howling with laughter, some scramble away from Jack as to not get covered in shit, others pull out their phones and record his downfall, while the smarter kids turn back around and mind their own business, clearly seeing the show is over.

But that's where they're wrong.

A member of our pack has been wronged and we don't let that shit slide.

Haven Falls Private is about to get a glimpse of their most feared pack in action.

As one, the four of us turn to face the football team. The fact that Tully was over there just a minute ago skanking around is completely forgotten. We all know where her loyalty is and it's right here, exactly where it belongs.

The whole group of football players sees the threat within the blink of an eye. We start walking forward. Some start backing away while confusion mars the faces of others. Only one is laced with fear and not a second later, he launches to his feet and races for the door.

He doesn't get far.

The whole fucking school has our back. We don't even need to break out into a jog. We take our fucking time knowing our school will deliver him to our feet. This is our show. Our stage. Our fucking fight.

We pull on our game faces. Each and every one of us looking hard as rock despite the fact that I know Tully is bursting at the seams, desperate to fist pump the sky because she'll get to knock some heads together.

Sensing this could turn into something more, our pack instinctively falls into formation; girls on the outside while Noah and Rivers take the middle, prepared and ready for any kind of brawl. After all, we're not ones to back down from a fight, no matter what kind of numbers are against us. Right now, we're facing down the whole football team and without a doubt in my mind, I know we'll win.

The guys near the door of the cafeteria get hold of Spencer and practically offer him up like a tasty little snack.

We stride forward. Purposeful and unbreakable.

We're fucking Untouchable.

I look straight ahead, past where Spencer is being deposited at our feet to the football team who all stand back. I fight a smirk. They're throwing Spencer to the wolves and claiming innocence. Our loyalty knows no bounds, whereas theirs is capped right before an ass whooping.

Spencer has never been more alone than in this moment and the second his eyes lock on Noah's, it's game fucking over.

Noah makes his move and let's hope for everyone's sake that Spencer learns his lesson this time.

Nobody fucks with our pack and gets away with it.

CHAPTER 8

"Miss Bronx," Mr. Carver says as the end of class bell sounds throughout the room. "Stay seated, please."

My eyes snap up to him at the front of the classroom. "What?" I whine as Tully looks across at me with drawn eyebrows. As a general rule, I only get asked to stay back when I've fucked up in some sort of way. And God's honest truth, I've been on my best behavior, especially after having Principal Evans' scream at the four of us the other day for our little performance in the cafeteria.

Noah received a two day suspension and I'm sure it would have been more if Evans was able to actually prove he did it. I mean, he had bleeding knuckles and everything, but not a damn person ratted him out. Not even Spencer.

Mr. Carver ignores my whines as he patiently waits for the classroom to clear out. "Guess I'll see you in a bit," Tully murmurs as she packs up her things and pushes up from her desk. "Just…whatever you do, don't admit to anything."

"I've got nothing to admit to. I haven't done anything."

"Henley," she sighs. "I highly doubt that. Now," she

adds, walking around the front of my desk and hugging her books to her chest. "Deny, deny, deny. And if in doubt, bat your lashes a little. He'll get confused and won't remember why he wants to hand your ass to you, and then you discreetly slip out."

I salute her. "Thanks, Captain. I'll keep that in mind."

Tully winks and gives me a wide grin. "That's my good little sea monster," she laughs before turning and striding out the door, leaving me surprised she didn't attempt to ruffle my hair.

The students pour out of the classroom and I turn my attention back to Mr. Carver as he plucks a few pieces of paper off his desk and pushes back out of his chair. He strides towards me and I pull on my game face in case this shit is about to go south.

My mind scrambles, desperately trying to think back over the past few days, going over every snide word or bitchy comment I've possibly made or even thought to make, but I come up blank. Apart from the Spencer shit, I've been a perfect little angel.

The door of the classroom is closed behind the last student, shutting out all the noise with it, leaving me and Carver in awkward silence.

He steps up before me and wordlessly places my paper down on my desk. My eyes instantly drop and rake over the paper. The first thing I notice is the bright red marker at the top reading 'A+.'

Holy shit. This is my test from the other day. I completely nailed it, but then, I shouldn't be surprised. I always nail my science tests. It's everything else that seems to go a little differently. But…why does he need to keep me after class to show me this? Normally, he just hands our tests back to us during class before going over it and explaining where we all went wrong as usually, the rest of the class seem to fail pretty badly.

"What are your plans for the future, Henley?" Mr. Carver

asks, sitting down on the desk in front of me.

I look up at him as confusion clouds my mind. "Ummm, what do you mean?" I question, wondering where the hell he could be going with this.

"What do you want to do after you graduate?" he clarifies. "Do you plan on attending college?"

I outright laugh at the poor guy. "I'm sorry," I say, trying to reign it in and focusing a little too hard on smothering my grin. I mean, is he for real right now? Surely, he understands what school he's been teaching in the past few years. "College? No one from Haven Falls goes to college."

"And why's that?" he questions, giving me a strange, challenging look.

I thought the whole no college for Haven Falls was a well-known thing, especially by the teachers or maybe he's actually asking my opinion. But then, maybe he's trying to have one of those 'serious' talks that teachers often like to give out to sound important and inspiring. "Because, it just doesn't happen," I tell him, not really having a proper answer for his question. "Haven Falls' kids don't belong in college. We can't afford it and we sure as hell don't get the grades to make it happen."

Mr. Carver nudges my test in front of me. "Really?" he questions. "Because that exam sitting in front of you says differently."

I glance down at the test, my eyes raking over the A+. "What are you trying to say?"

"I'm saying that you're selling yourself short," he tells me before waiting a short moment, watching me curiously. "What is it that you want to do with your life, Henley? And don't give me the bullshit answer that you most likely gave the guidance counselor."

"I…," I glance away.

"You want to study science in a professional capacity, don't you?"

I bite the inside of my cheek, terrified that he's trying to fill me with false hope. "What makes you say that?"

"Apart from the fact that I see what you're like in my class, I looked up your grades," he admits. "And you know what I found? They absolutely suck." My eyes shoot up at him, ready to jump on the defense. "Yet, here you are getting A's or A pluses on every one of my exams. Science intrigues you. I see the way you focus in class. I see your eyes light up each time we discuss an experiment. This is something you want, you just don't know how to get it."

I can hardly focus on what he's saying. I don't like where he's going with this. This is a setup, one that could only cause me to fail and feel like shit about myself.

"You have the potential to make something of yourself, Henley," he continues, "You're throwing it away because of some ridiculous stereotypical bullshit that kids from Haven Falls preach to make failing acceptable." He scoffs as though the very thought offends him. "Well, guess what?" he adds. "If you want it and you actually put a little effort into your classes, there's no reason why you shouldn't be able to get into a good college. Broken Hill University to be exact. They have a great science program."

I shake my head. This is too much. "Thanks for the thought, but you're forgetting one little, very important thing."

He waves his hand in front of himself, indicating for me to go on. "Please, do share."

"College is expensive, and I don't know about you, but in my household, a bit of spare cash means the bills get paid on time and I don't have to shower in cold water. I know you haven't been teaching here that long, but to the kids of Haven Falls, having a college fund is as rare as winning the freaking jackpot."

Carver slides another piece of paper in front of me with a knowing glint in his eye. "What if I told you there was a way?"

He's got to be nuts, right?

I look down at the paper and read over it. Surely, I'm not seeing this right. A scholarship? What the hell? I suck in a breath. "What is this?"

"It's exactly what you think it is. You have the potential to be better than Haven Falls. Right now, you're letting your town dictate who you can be and how far in life you can go. Step outside of the box, Henley. I see so much more in you than waiting tables at Whataburger."

I look down again. Hardly able to believe what I'm seeing. A freaking scholarship. Am I even eligible for this? No, it's not possible. Not with my grades. I mean, my science grades are outstanding, but everything else? No, there's just no way.

"What do you want to study, Henley?" Carver asks me softly. "And don't even think about lying. I'm the one who grades all of your exams, I know when a topic interest you.

I bite down on my bottom lip before looking up at him and letting out a breath. What's the harm in sharing? If anything, he could maybe add in a few more lessons on the topic. "Genetic Genealogy," I tell him. "I don't know, something about human DNA intrigues me. It's fascinating and complex while so freaking straight forward at the same time."

"It sure is," he agrees with a proud smile before getting up from the desk, though I don't know what he's proud about, all I did was tell him something about myself. It's not as though I just received an acceptance letter.

"Look," Carver says, glancing down at the application form under my fingers. "Think it over and if it's something you really want; I will help you apply and speak with your teachers about putting together a plan to help raise your grades. There's a future for you here, I promise you that," he adds. "You just have to see it and want it bad enough to make it happen."

Well, shit. That's not how I expected my afternoon to go.

I nod my head, unable to form any words as I continue staring at the paper before me that could promise a whole different life, one I never expected could have even been a possibility. "Get out of here, Henley," Carver says, probably not even realizing the weight he's just dropped on my shoulders. "Go get yourself some lunch and think over your options."

"Ok," I say, pushing up from my desk and grabbing my things before taking the scholarship application between my fingers. "Thanks for this. I, uhh…I'll let you know."

Mr. Carver nods his head before stepping back and excusing me.

I walk out of his classroom, hardly able to make sense of the thoughts running through my mind. I've never even bothered to consider college because it's simply a luxury we can't afford, but a scholarship…that would change everything. My only issue is making myself want it and working towards it, only to not receive it. That would be devastating and all the hard work I'll have to do until graduation would all be for nothing.

I mean, not completely for nothing. There's always room for a better education and receiving knowledge but to not get that scholarship; that would kill me.

I make my way down to the cafeteria on autopilot, not really seeing a damn thing around me. Pushing through the door, I spot Noah, Tully, and Rivers almost instantly. All three sets of eyes fly to mine with concern and I realize Tully probably explained that I was in shit.

Little do they know, Tully was right. I am in shit, just a different kind then what they're expecting.

Seeing the concern on Noah's face, the fog begins to clear. I walk forward and drop down by his side as Tully leans forward on the table, peering around Noah's side to get a better look at me. "What happened?" she questions, not blessing me with a second to work out how to word this.

I look up at her and I can't help but grin, knowing exactly how she's going to react to this. "Carver thinks I should be applying to college."

Tully instantly booms out with laughter as Noah raises a brow in curiosity. "Why would he think that?" Noah prompts, realizing there's a little more to this story than just an opportunity to mock our disgraceful standards.

"Because I seem to have a bit of a…gift when it comes to science."

Tully scoffs beside her brother. "That's a bit of an understatement," she says. "She's like a fucking science nerd. That shit gets her hot." She nudges Noah's elbow. "You should probably screw her in the science labs. I'd bet all the money in the world that she'd go off like a bomb in there," Tully winks. "You can thank me later."

Noah just raises his brow once again as Rivers watches on in silence. "Is that true?" Noah asks. "You've never told me that."

"Why would I?" I laugh. "It's not like you're here telling me all about the fucking shit you were building during shop. If I start talking about that I'm either going to confuse that pretty little head of yours or send you into a coma out of pure boredom." Noah rolls his eyes but I continue before he can disagree. "Besides, what does it matter? After graduation, that's it. School will be over and we'll probably never talk about it again."

Noah continues watching me and it feels like his gaze is digging deep within me. "You want to go though, don't you?"

"Come on," I laugh. "College is like a distant dream that no one from Haven Falls has the right to even think about. You know that just as well as I do."

"So, why would Carver bother bringing it up with you?" Rivers questions, finally adding a little something to the conversation while sounding extremely confused about it all.

I shrug my shoulders and consider not showing them the scholarship application. If I don't talk about it, then it's not really real, right? If I don't apply and don't work my ass off for it, then there's no chance of getting my hopes crushed when they pick someone else. It's the safest option, but Carver is right, if I was to do that, I'd be selling myself short.

I groan before letting out a heavy sigh. "He wants me to apply for a scholarship," I say, grabbing the application form off my lap and sliding it in front of Noah. "He thinks I have the potential to get it if I can increase my grades in all my other classes."

Tully's eyes widen in surprise. "Shit. Really?" she grunts. "He's not fucking with you?"

"Nope," I say as I watch Noah reading closely over the application, so close that anyone would think it's the only lifeline standing between him and a million dollars.

Noah grunts without taking his eyes from the papers. "You'd be a fucking idiot not to try."

I look away from him. From everyone. "Yeah...but."

Noah looks up at my tone and turns to face me, somehow managing to block out Tully and Rivers so it's only us in this moment. "But what, Spitfire?"

My baby blues meet his stormy greens and all my troubles come pouring out like word vomit. "I just...what if I start pulling my shit together and working my ass off for it and then don't get it? It would all be for nothing and I'll feel like absolute shit. But then, what if I do get it? Dad couldn't handle Aria all the time. He wouldn't be able to work."

"You're thinking too much into it, babe. Broken Hill University is a fifteen minute drive away and it's not like you'd be in classes from sun up to sun down. You'll have a schedule and your dad could work around it, and if not, you've always got us. I could pick up Aria from school. She'd fucking love it. She'd show off to all her friends thinking she's badass."

"She is badass," I grumble under my breath as I consider everything he's saying.

"Besides," Noah continues, "no one is about to deny you that scholarship."

"How do you know that?"

"Because I'll be down there kicking some asses until they accept it."

I roll my eyes. "You can't do that," I tell him with a groan. "If I'm going to do this, if I'm going to get in then I want to know I earned it because I worked my ass off, not because my scary as shit boyfriend threatened some old rich guy in a suit."

"Hey," Rivers cuts in. "You'd be surprised. The old rich guys aren't exactly easily swayed. Noah would have to put up a pretty big fight. Trust me, I know."

I ignore Rivers comments as a reminder of what he and Noah do isn't exactly going to help calm my screaming mind right now. "Noah?" I prompt. "Promise me. If I do this, I do it on my own."

His eyes soften as he leans in and slides his hands into place on my thighs. "Promise," he whispers.

Noah's forehead rests against mine and I let out a breath. "You're lying," I murmur, knowing him better than I know myself.

He shrugs his shoulders, completely unfazed by being caught out lying. "What can I say?" he grins, unapologetically. "You're my girl and I fucking love you. I'm not about to stand back and not even try to give you the world. If this is what you want, then you can bet your ass I'll make it happen."

Jesus. It's not like that is even in his realm of capabilities. "You realize this is a scholarship into a rich person college, not jacking a car? I mean, your manipulation game is strong, but it's not that strong."

"I got you, didn't I?" he says with a cheesy as fuck grin.

"You're an idiot."

"And you're going to be a college student."

"We'll see," I mutter.

"Uh huh," he says, pulling away from me and pulling a pen out of who the hell knows where before he starts filling out my application.

"What are you doing?" I screech, pulling at his arm.

Noah shakes me off and Rivers and Tully laugh in amusement. "Shut up," Noah scolds. "I'm busy."

I groan and let him do his thing. He's most likely going to fill it out wrong anyway meaning I'll have to start over, but if it makes him feel like a fucking boss doing it, then by all means, he can destroy the form as much as he wants.

Tully laughs on the other side of Noah and I glance up to find her face shoved into her phone as she busily texts someone. Rivers eyes narrow on her, knowing that with the four of us sitting at the table, there's not many other people she could be texting, especially people who could make her laugh.

"Who the fuck you textin'?" Rivers grunts.

Tully's head snaps up with a ferocious glare as Noah groans beside me. "That's none of your goddamn business," Tully scowls at him.

I didn't think it was possible but Rivers eyes somehow narrow on her even more and then in the blink of an eye, his arm flies across the table and snatches her phone out of her unexpecting hands, shocking us all. "No," Tully screeches as Rivers scans over the text. "Give me my phone, asshole."

Rivers face turns a deep shade of red as he slams her phone down on the table, most likely smashing the screen as students all through the cafeteria whip their heads in our direction. "Like fuck you're going out with Rocko tomorrow night."

"I'll go out with whoever the hell I want," she throws right back at him. "You lost your right to have any say over my love life when you fucked us up."

Noah's head snaps up, all thoughts of college application forms gone as he stares at Rivers. "What the fuck is that supposed to mean?"

Tully shoots to her feet, still scowling at Rivers as she responds to her brother. "Nothing. It means absolutely nothing." With that, she storms out of the cafeteria and not a second later, Rivers disappears in the opposite direction, leaving Noah and I sitting behind in complete silence.

CHAPTER 9

"Can you believe that fucking idiot?" Tully demands as we walk through the campus of Broken Hill University.

"I know," I tell her, not bothering to expand on my outrage as this is probably the twentieth time we've discussed it since lunch. Both Tully and Rivers disappeared and with everything going to shit for the afternoon, Noah and I left right behind them, skipping the rest of class for the day. I mean, it's not exactly a good start to the whole 'trying to get my grades up for college' but our pack was in meltdown mode and we couldn't just ignore that.

I get lost looking around at all the fancy ass buildings and realize this place looks way too major leagues for me. It's freaking beautiful and screams money. I don't belong here. I'd feel like a fraud getting a free ride to a place like this, but then, it would be the most moronic thing to turn it down if I was lucky enough to be accepted.

Crap. I knew when Kaylah suggested coming here tonight for Jackson's football game, I should have rejected the offer. All this is going to do is make my head spin with unanswered questions. Either that or it's going to make me see a future that is so far beyond my reach and that's only going to cut me down if it doesn't happen.

I'm setting myself up for failure. My hopes will be crushed, but Noah assures me that he's got this.

That idiot. He might be Superman but he's not a fucking magician. Only I can make it happen. If Noah went in there blazing with his threats and tough guy persona, he'll get laughed out and I'll lose whatever shot I had. I have to do this on my own and the only way little ol' me is going to get noticed is by pulling some killer grades out of my ass.

Damn. That requires studying.

After finding Tully sulking this afternoon, I needed something to get her mind off it. I called Kaylah thinking she could come over to my place and we could have a girls' night with Aria. Nails, hair, movie, and popcorn. It would have been great. Dad would have locked himself in his bedroom and not come out until the coast was clear, but the second Kaylah said she had promised Jackson that she'd come to his game, Tully was on her feet getting ready.

I had no freaking choice.

Tully thought it was a great idea, you know, give me a chance to see the school and hopefully convince me that this scholarship is the right way to go. I mean, I don't need much convincing. All their arguments are too good and all my excuses are complete shit.

Noah's right, I'd be a fool not to give this my all. This could mean a future that I never thought possible for myself. I can just see it now, the first Haven Falls girl to make something of herself. Well, I guess that's not fair. Many of the women from Haven Falls have been successful, but I doubt any of them have done it with a college degree.

The more I've been thinking about it, the more I feel that Tully should be giving the whole college thing a crack too. She could do a business degree which would give her all the tools to make her floristry business a raging success.

She could take an online floristry course, learn a little about marketing and communications, maybe even a little bookkeeping course, and she'd be set.

Me, though? College? Wow.

Henley Meadow Bronx; Professor. Yeah, I freaking like it.

The more I think about it, the more I want it and that's kind of scaring the shit out of me.

Damn it. I have to start thinking about something else before I send myself crazy. I loop my arm through Tully's. "You need to distract me," I tell her. "All this college bullshit is going to make me scream and it's not going to be pretty."

Tully scoffs. "You really think I'm capable of distracting you without bringing up Rivers or Rocko right now?"

"Good point," I laugh. "What did the boys end up doing tonight?"

"I don't know," she shrugs. "You'd have a better idea than I would. I haven't heard from either of them since school. My guess is that Noah went looking for Rivers, and Rivers is hiding out somewhere to avoid explaining what the fuck that was all about."

"Good point," I say, pulling my phone out once again to find nothing from Noah. I haven't spoken to him since we left school. He dropped me off at his place assuming Tully was there and went to go find Rivers, but that was hours ago.

If he found him and managed to get anything out of him, I'd dare say the two boys are covered head to toe in blood and bruises. If he hasn't found him, Noah will be at home, punching holes in walls as his mind goes over all the possibilities of what would have made Tully say something like that.

Not freaking good.

Noah's probably going through all kinds of hell right now and I'm here, about to watch some stupid football game. Great girlfriend I am.

Well, to be honest, I doubt we'll be watching anything. We've been walking around this damn campus for twenty minutes and still haven't found the stadium. Maybe neither of us are smart enough to go to college after all.

I hear the roar of the crowd. In fact, we've been hearing it since we got here. I assumed we'd park the car and follow the crowd, but we must have parked in the wrong place because there sure as hell isn't a crowd to follow.

A call comes through on my phone and I glance down to find Kaylah's name written across the screen. I answer almost instantly.

"Are you guys still coming?" she yells down the line, probably struggling to hear with the noise of the crowd behind her.

"Yeah," I say, hoping I'm speaking loud enough for her. "We've been here a while. I think we're lost."

A chuckle comes out of her. "Really?" she questions with amusement deep in her voice.

"Yes," I groan before looking around at where we are. "We're on campus. Out front of the Macquarie Library."

"Shit," she laughs. "Why the hell are you there? You're completely in the wrong place." Kaylah gives us a few directions and I start pulling Tully in the opposite direction before ending the call with Kaylah.

After another ten minutes of walking, we finally find the stadium, and it is fucking huge.

How could we have missed this?

We head for the ticket booth and get ourselves sorted before making our way inside the huge stadium. My mouth drops open. This is freaking incredible.

Pride surges through me. This is all Jackson has ever talked about and he did it. He made it to the big leagues and I don't doubt that by the end of college, he'll be leaving with a contract to the NFL. He's just that good.

Tully and I make our way up the massive grandstand,

still following the directions Kaylah had given us. She's saved some seats for us amongst her friends, wanting us to have the absolute best time of our lives.

I curse myself for still not being able to memorize all of Kaylah's friends' names. One day I'll remember them. I mean, I've pretty much got Nate, Jesse, and Tora down, but the rest…they're kind of a blur in my mind. Why is it that I only seem to meet them when I've been drinking?

"There you are," Kaylah squeals as we make our way across the row, squeezing in front of the annoyed spectators who managed to make it on time and not get lost. "Hurry up. It's just about to start."

I drag Tully behind me and we find our seats just as the teams are rushing out onto the field amongst a bunch of the hottest cheerleaders I've ever seen. I mean, shit. The cheerleaders at Haven Falls are nothing like this. I'm used to plastic, bimbo bitches with bad attitudes, but these ones, they're just…hot. They're real. Who knows, they could be plastic and most likely are bitches, but they have an air of realness around them.

Maybe that's just what happens when you graduate from high school. You suddenly have to grow the fuck up and leave all the bullshit high school drama behind. I can't freaking wait for that.

I lean across Kaylah and say 'hey' to Jesse and one of his friends who I'm pretty sure is Tyson. Jackson's girlfriend, Elle, is on the other side of Tyson and gives me and Tully a warm smile before I give up on saying 'hi' to the rest. Tora, Nate, and some other dude are too far down the line and I'd have to scream over the sound of the crowd to get their attention. Not worth it. I'll catch them at half time.

As the game goes on, I can't help but watch Jackson just like I always used to. Only this time it's different. Instead of studying the way his body moves and how incredible he looks in his uniform, I'm watching just how good he is. He's only new to the team and I'm sure there are a few others who want to remind him of that, but don't be fooled, by the end of the season the whole world will know he's a fucking star, just as Kaylah and I have always known.

Before I know it, we've been here for nearly two hours without even the slightest thought of Noah or Rivers. The buzzer sounds and Tully and I stand on our feet, cheering for Jackson's team as they've absolutely dominated the game. They shake hands with the opposing team in a show of good sportsmanship before jumping around the fucking field like idiots.

We start making our way out of the row and I fall into easy conversation with the Broken Hill kids as we wait for Jackson to finish up with his team.

Twenty minutes later, Jackson shows his pretty face and Elle rushes up to him before throwing herself up into his arms. Jesse and Tyson groan about 'saving it for later' while the rest of us crowds around him to say congratulations.

"Hey, what the hell are you doing here?" Jackson beams, pulling me into a tight hug against his hard chest before ruffling my hair like a little sister.

"Ugh, get off me," I say, scrunching up my face before pushing against his chest, not getting the same thrill from being in his arms that I used to. I straighten up my hair and look up at him as I answer his question. I indicate towards Tully. "We needed a distraction so Kaylah thought it'd be a good chance to come check out the campus and get our minds off...things."

His eyes narrow. "What things? Noah didn't hurt you, did he?"

"No," I scoff, practically laughing at the absurdity of Noah hurting me. "The furthest from it. The idiot is trying to convince me to apply for a scholarship here."

Jackson's brows practically disappear into his hairline. "You? A scholarship? For what? The last I checked, you wouldn't even know what an 'A' was," he teases, completely forgetting about the fact that he was digging for information as to why we would need an escape from home. Though, it's not like I'm about to tell him all about Tully and Rivers' issues.

I playfully smack his arm but roll my eyes. Getting teased by Jackson Millington isn't exactly a new thing for me. "Shut up."

Kaylah butts in on our conversation with a teasing grin of her own. "She's a science nerd, remember?"

Jackson studies me a moment before it all comes back to him. "That's right," he says, proudly. "You're all into DNA and that shit."

"Uh huh."

"Shit," he chuckles. "How could I have forgotten about that?"

Well, forgetting shit about people that you completely abandon for eight months tends to have that effect on a person, but I wouldn't dare say that out loud. It's still a bit of a sore point for us all.

I mean, I figured I was completely over it, but the fact that the thought just popped into my head suggests otherwise.

"Wait," Jackson says, the grin suddenly disappearing from his face. "Why would Noah be trying to convince you to apply for a scholarship? Why the hell aren't you jumping at the opportunity?" I glance away, forgetting that Jackson has been able to read me like a map for years. "Ahhhh, you're shit scared."

My eyes instantly zone back in on his. "I'm not fucking scared," I shoot back at him.

He watches me with a "Prove it, chicken."

I resist smacking him in the face.

My scowl is sharp enough to cut glass. How dare he call me a chicken. Out of all the people in my life, he's one of the few who know me well enough to know I'm no fucking chicken.

We continue staring each other down. "What's holding you back, Henley?" I keep my mouth shut. Like hell I'm about to admit my insecurities and fears in front of a bunch of people I hardly know. But once again, he reads me like a fucking map. He lowers his voice to keep our conversation a little more private. "You can't let the fear of failure dictate your life, babe."

"I'm not."

"You are. You're terrified of getting your hopes up and then having some pretentious ass take it all away by saying that you're not good enough. The kind of person who isn't good enough is the kind of person not willing to give it a shot," he says. "Do you really think I'd be here, winning fucking college games if I didn't take a shot on myself and stayed on a losing team at Haven Falls? No fucking way. You don't get what you want without working for it, Henley."

"But…"

"No, don't give me your fucking excuses. You're applying for it whether or not you like it. If you get it, fucking awesome. If you don't, search out your other options, but either way, you're not going to fall into the Haven Falls stereotype. You're going to be something, Henley. I can feel it."

I roll my eyes. "Jesus," I chuckle. "No need for the dramatics."

"Yes, there is," he tells me. "I can already see the fire growing in your eyes. You want to prove me wrong for calling you a chicken."

"Challenge fucking accepted," I laugh. "I ain't no chicken."

"Like I said," he grins. "Prove it."

And just like that, it looks like I'm going to need a brand new application form.

"Come on," Jackson says, taking Elle's hand and dropping his heavy arm over my shoulder. "Let me take you for a tour around campus. See if I can really change your mind."

Tully loops her arm through mine and before I know it, we're walking through campus, both of us in awe, realizing a future we never knew we wanted.

An hour later, we find ourselves at Tora's place attending our first college party on a Thursday night of all nights. I mean, who the hell parties on a Thursday night?

The party flies by while Tully and I have the time of our lives. If Jackson's lecture and the campus tour wasn't enough to convince me that I should be applying for that scholarship, then this party certainly is.

CHAPTER 10

After drinking way too much to drive ourselves home, Jackson's over the top, brotherly protectiveness comes shooting out as he ushers us out of Tora's place and to his car. He even grabs Kaylah and hauls her out too, saying it's way too late for her to be staying much longer on a school night. I mean, come on!

Jesse has a few choice words to say about Jackson's protective tendencies, but he puts up a good fight and before we know it, even Jesse is walking out the door and heading for his Range Rover, offering to take Kaylah so Jackson doesn't have to make too many stops.

I don't know how Jackson does it. He must be some kind of kickass manipulator. I'm pretty sure he even had Jesse thinking it was his decision to head home, and believe me, I have a feeling Jesse has never left a party at this hour in his life. He's generally the guy who's still partying while people are waking up around him and getting the place cleaned up before their parents get home. I can only imagine what people must go through when it's time to tell a guy like Jesse

Ryder to go home.

Tully and I drop down into Jackson's black Charger and I smile at all the fond memories I've had in this car. Jackson taught me how to drive a stick shift in this thing. Now, they are some memories that I should probably try to forget. Learning to drive wasn't exactly the easiest thing. Dad was gone most of the time and so I basically taught myself in the old pick up truck. Believe me, it wasn't pretty.

When Jackson realized what a shitty job I was doing, he stepped in and taught me. Having such a nasty crush on him at the time, I didn't get much concentrating done, add that to the fact that I was teaching myself to drive in an ancient truck, and I nearly sent us hurtling onto the boardwalk and into the ocean. Trust me when I say there's a huge difference between driving a car like Jackson's and driving something older than my dad.

Jackson didn't let me drive much after that.

Noah's Camaro though, that's as easy as riding Noah himself. You just got to show it who's boss and it will come alive beneath you, letting you feel its deep rumble and smooth, harder edges. Pure perfection.

"What's going on in that head of yours?" Jackson questions, pulling me out of my thoughts as he drives towards Haven Falls.

I blink a few times, hardly remembering where the hell I am. I quickly glance back at Tully and find her laying across the backseat, using Jackson's old high school letterman jacket as a pillow, making a fond smile pull at my lips. "Nothing," I say, turning back to the front to give her a little privacy as she drools all over the jacket and grumbles in her sleep.

"Bullshit," Jackson chuckles to himself before quickly glancing across at me. "I've known you forever, Henley. You were having dirty thoughts and you can't fucking deny it."

"What?" I gasp, sucking in a breath and gawking at him. I mean, a few dirty thoughts kind of surfaced in my mind, but this guy doesn't need to know about them and he sure as hell doesn't need to know that the second I walk through the door of Noah's bedroom, it will be locking behind me and not opening until I've had my fill of him. "I was not having dirty thoughts."

Jackson raises a brow, once again challenging me and I try to think back to what was going through my mind before it was assaulted with all things Noah. It finally comes back to me - his stupid car and the stupid boardwalk. "I was just remembering when you taught me how to drive stick shift in this thing," I tell him, relieved that it's a topic that should distract him from the last one.

"Oh, yeah. You fucking sucked," he laughs. "Are you still a shit driver? I bet you are."

"Excuse you," I say. "I'll have you know that I am fucking awesome. I could whip your ass any day on the track."

"Right," he grins.

"Rumor has it that it's not that hard to beat you anyway." I start counting my fingers. "How many times has Nate beaten you now? Shit, I don't have enough hands to work that one out."

His head whips my way as he narrows his eyes on mine. "Take that back."

I shrug my shoulders. "Sorry, I just can't," I say as a thought hits me. "Have you ever raced Noah?"

Jackson sinks back into his chair as he falls into deep thought. "I don't think I have," he tells me. "But I sure as hell can beat his ass."

"Right," I say, mimicking his earlier tone.

We fall into easy conversation the rest of the way back to Noah's place and I can't help but feel comfortable with how easy it comes. It's almost as though I truly have my old friend back. I've missed this and it's so much better because the swirling thoughts in my head are completely gone. Well, that's not entirely true, there are still swirling thoughts in my head, but they're just not about him. Not anymore and never will be again.

Noah has completely consumed me. Never in my wildest dream would I think that I was lucky enough to find a guy like Noah, and I certainly never thought that he'd fall in love with me and completely sweep me off my feet. I must be living in some kind of alternate universe because shit like that just doesn't happen, but I'll be damned if I don't hold onto it as tight as I can. Surely, time is going to run out on me soon and I want to have made the most of it when that time comes.

I really hope that time never comes. I'm having way too much fun. Being Noah's girl, shit. Noah's girl. I still can't get used to that. Being his girl is an absolute dream come true. He's wormed his way under my hard exterior and is taking away the darkness within.

I always assumed that being in love with someone made you soft and reliant, but I was so damn wrong. He lifts me up. He continues to let me be independent. In fact, he soars seeing me taking care of myself, but no matter what, he'll be close by in case I need him. He'll never let me fall, but he'll sure as hell let me learn from my mistakes just as I do for him.

He reads my body. He knows when I need him by my side and he knows when I need to stand on my own two feet. That couldn't possibly be a trait that all men possess. If it were, I have a feeling the world would be a happier place.

Jackson pulls up at Noah's place and I realize that easy conversation we had fallen into was completely deserted by my girly daydreaming about Noah...again. How is that possible?

I get myself out of his car and walk around to the back door to help get Tully out. God, this is going to be hard. I hope she's not too hard to wake up. The last time this happened, we nearly crashed into the mailbox when she dropped all her weight on me. It wasn't pretty.

"No," Jackson says, pushing out of the driver's door and coming around the back. "Don't wake her. I'll take her in."

"Thanks," I say, grateful. "Waking Tully isn't exactly a

pretty thing."

He looks down at her and takes in the drool on his jacket. "Yeah, I can imagine."

Jackson grabs her ankles and pulls her along until she's at the edge of the seat, making her hair and arms splay out across the backseat. He ducks down and scoops her into his arms before pulling her out of the car.

I duck in once they're out of the way and feel around the floor of the car until I find her phone, shoes, and purse. Once I'm sure I have everything, I lead Jackson up the pathway towards the front door.

It opens before I have a chance to do it myself and I look up at Rivers who watches Jackson and Tully with a deep scowl before he steps forward and holds out his arms, demanding, not asking, Jackson to hand over the precious goods.

Not wanting to ruffle any feathers, Jackson happily hands her over and bows out. He says a quick goodnight and before I know it, I'm hurrying down the hallway, passing Rivers in order to open Tully's bedroom door before he reaches it.

I rush in, pull down her blankets, and toss her things on the floor beside her bed before leaving the rest up to Rivers. I'm sure come morning when Tully realizes Rivers was the one to put her to bed, she'll probably have a few words to say about it, but I also have a feeling that Rivers would kick my ass if I suggested he leave right now.

On my way to Noah's room, I stop by the bathroom to pee and wash off my makeup before deciding to search the cupboard for a spare toothbrush. I probably smell like a bar after the night I've had and I doubt that's really going to be the biggest turn on, though, I doubt Noah would ever say no. He never says no. No matter what.

As I push my way into Noah's room, I find him sitting up in bed, his arm behind his head and his phone in hand. The light is off but the lamp post out front of their home is enough for me to see the perfect ridges of his abs.

His eyes turn on mine with a fondness that has me walking towards him. "I didn't think you'd be coming here tonight."

I shrug my shoulders. "Dad's home with Aria and Tully needed someone to stay with her, besides, why the hell wouldn't I want to come here and spend the night in your bed?"

A grin stretches across his lips as he pulls me down onto his bed. "And don't you fucking forget it," he tells me, dropping his lips to mine. "Where the hell were you guys?" he questions out of curiosity. "I haven't heard from either of you since school."

"Sorry," I murmur against his lips. "It took me forever to get Tully to finally quit complaining about Rivers and then Kaylah invited us to go to Jackson's football game at BHU."

"Jackson, huh?" he says, pulling back with a strange darkness in his eyes. "Tell me, why does his name keep coming up?"

I bring my hand up and trace my fingers over his perfect lips. "You're not jealous, are you?" I tease. "Just wait until you find out that we went to a party with him, got a little too drunk, and then let him drive us home, but that was before we let him take advantage of us in the backseat."

Noah's eyes narrow on me and he certainly doesn't look impressed. It doesn't take a genius to work out that he's waiting for an explanation, but I make him sweat it. "How was your night?" I question, feigning innocence.

"Henley," he snaps, hating the thoughts that are undoubtedly clouding his mind.

"Fine," I laugh. "Trust me, it was all coincidental. I called Kaylah and told her about the scholarship and said we needed a girls' night, but she was already going to the game and said that it would be fun if we go and that it would give me a chance to see the college, so, we went," I explain. "Oh, and the game was awesome by the way. Jackson's team killed it."

"Get to the getting drunk with your ex shit."

"He's not my ex," I clarify.

"You know what I fucking mean."

"I like it when you get jealous," I grin. "It's kind of sexy."

"Nothing about me is just 'kind of sexy'. It's all or nothing," he clarifies. "Now, get the fuck on with it."

I can't help but raise my head to kiss him once again. "After the game, we stayed to say 'hi', you know, being polite and all that. I mentioned the scholarship and he thought that giving us a tour of the campus would help convince me to apply."

"Did it?" he questions.

My cheeks puff up so damn much that my eyes end up squinting into tiny little slits. "Yeah," I tell him. "That school is fucking awesome. It reeks of money, but I felt important being there like I was meant for more than just Haven Falls. I feel like I have a purpose now."

His eyes soften and it's almost as though he forgets about Jackson for just a moment, the shortest, tiniest, little moment. "Do you have any idea how fucking happy that makes me?" he murmurs, grabbing my waist and rolling us until I hover above him.

I smile down at him, loving the sound of those words on my ears. His happiness is like a drug to me and that's another thing I've had to get used to. I always thought that only my happiness mattered. This world is about doing things for yourself, but I'm quickly realizing how wrong that is. "I thought it might," I tell him.

"The party, Spitfire," he prompts.

I push up on his chest and look down at his magnificent body, the dull light streaming through his bedroom window making it all that much better. "Who cares about the party?" I groan, reaching the hem of my shirt and pulling it over my head. "We've got much more important things to be doing right now."

Noah's hands instantly take my waist as his eyes roam

over my body. His hands begin to roam, and I suck in a breath when one travels down to my ass, getting a good feel and desperately making me wish I'd taken my jeans off already. His hand is there one second, and the next, it's coming down hard on my ass, giving it a good spanking. "The party," he prompts again.

"Fine," I grumble. "But promise you'll let me make it up to you afterward?"

"Babe, like I could fucking resist you right now," he tells me, pressing his hips up into me and letting me know that whether or not I answer him right now, we'll both be getting away with something tonight.

Feeling his hardness beneath me has me grinding down into him and closing my eyes with pure satisfaction. "You know Tora?" I ask, sliding my hands up his strong chest.

"Mmm."

"We went to her place with all the Broken Hill guys," I explain. "It was supposed to be just us, but you know how it is when Jesse and Nate go anywhere."

"It turns into a fucking party," he chuckles, taking the very words right out of my mouth.

"Uh huh," I say, coming down to brush my lips across his, desperately needing that closeness and the feel of his warm breath against my skin. "But don't worry. With the Ryders', their friends, and Jackson there, Tully and I couldn't even pee without one of them hovering over us."

"Good," he grumbles, grinding himself up into me once again. "How is Tully? Has she calmed down yet?"

I drop my face down to his neck and kiss his neck, tasting his sweet skin. "You really want to talk about your sister right now?" I question.

Noah's hand slides down into the back of my jeans, grabbing a handful of ass and the other hand trails up my back and effortless unhooks my bra with one quick flick of his fingers. "You're fucking right," he murmurs, taking the lead.

My bra comes off before he quickly rolls us until I'm flat on my back and he's knelt between my legs, his hands working the button of my jeans. Noah rids them off my body and it's like he can't be with me fast enough.

He falls back down to me, our bodies crashing together as his lips devour mine, his tongue slipping in and making my tummy swirl with anticipation, knowing that whatever he's got in store for me is going to be good.

His big hand slides up my body and cups my breast before giving it a squeeze that has my stomach clenching. I need more than that. So much more.

Noah grins against my lips and a second later, he's gone. I almost cry out for him when I feel his lips replacing his hand on my breast. His tongue runs over my pebbled nipple and has me arching up into him as my nails dig into his back.

I swear, this man must have endless claw marks all over him. I feel kind of bad for him, but then, I kind of don't.

I'm so taken by what he's doing with his tongue that I don't notice his hand heading south until it's already there. Touching. Kneading. Rubbing. Fucking everything I could possibly need and more.

He works my body to the edge and as I reach for him, he pulls back with a shake of his head, showing off that body of his once again, but now I can hardly concentrate. All I can look at is the huge outline of his dick through his jeans and believe me when I say he is more than happy to see me.

"Nuh uh, Spitfire," he says with a 'tsk' as his hand goes to the top of his unbuttoned jeans, teasing me with what hides beneath. "You're going to have to wait for this. You've been a very bad girl and I'm going to have to teach you a lesson to remind you to never do it again."

"But what if I like being a bad girl?"

His eyes flame with desire. "Believe me, Spitfire. There's more than one way to punish you."

Fuck me. I think my eyes roll to the back of my head. Maybe I pass out for a moment too.

"You better get on with it, Noah," I tell him. "You've got me all worked up and if you're not careful, I'll have to do it myself."

His eyes roam over my body with a shit eating grin. "By all means, baby. I'm down for a show."

Fuck. That backfired.

As if sensing the desperation within me, he gives me mercy as his lips come back to mine. He doesn't waste a second. He gets back to teasing my body with his practiced moves, not once giving me a second to cool down. The longer he goes, the hotter my body becomes but the more I crave the feel of his.

I need his skin on mine. I need his touch. His lips. His everything.

My hands trail down his strong back, feeling every tight muscle on the way down. They trace over the small dimples on his lower back until they're slipping under the fabric of his jeans, feeling that perfect ass and pushing his jeans down.

If he's not going to give me what I need soon, then he better fucking believe that I'll take it for myself.

The fire burns just as strongly with him and I thank my lucky stars when he helps me push his jeans the rest of the way down his legs until they're kicked off the end of his bed. He kisses me deeply as he grabs my legs, separating them until he's comfortably between them.

With a hand on my ass, the other wrapped around my ribs and his mouth devouring my nipple, he finally gives in, pushing up into me until I'm seeing stars and reminding me that I'm his fucking queen. Now and forever.

CHAPTER 11

Noah pulls up at school on Friday morning and with a few extra minutes before the bell, we find ourselves sitting in his car, me devouring a coffee as he scrolls through Facebook, though, from the disinterested look on his face, I'd dare say he's not finding anything to hold his attention.

I glance down and can't help but smile as I take in Noah's hand in mine with his thumb unconsciously running back and forth over my knuckles. I love the way he loves me. He probably doesn't even realize that he's doing it. It's just his body's natural reaction, its basic instinct when I'm around. Hell, I'm sure that I have little quirks like that which Noah has picked up on that I'm not aware of.

I woke up in his arms this morning and the first thing I noticed was the feel of his body against mine. I was so freaking happy in that moment. It's not often that I get to wake up with his arms wrapped around me. The next thing I noticed was his morning wood. Even in his sleep, he's happy to see me.

A yawn ripped through me which was when it truly hits

me. Absolute horror. I'd spent the night at Noah's place, sleeping in his warm arms and completely forgetting to let my father know what was going on.

Shit. That could only mean one thing.

Fucking trouble.

I scrambled over Noah and accidentally kneed him in the balls as I reached for my phone. The movement only managing to remind me that I'd had one too many cocktails at Tora's party the night before.

I got my phone and lit up the screen to find nothing. Nada. Zilch.

My father is notorious for overreacting when I don't come home, so to see an empty screen wasn't exactly settling. It could mean a few different things.

One; he's still fast asleep and didn't realize I'm still not home. Unlikely.

Two; he'd been up panicking all night to the point I put him in a stress induced coma, leaving him physically unable to assault me through text messages. More likely than the sleeping shit.

Three; he's finally realized the boys are never going to let me get hurt so he's finally chilled out. Again, unlikely.

Four; he's completely given up on me, hoping it's not too late to mold Aria into the perfect daughter who wouldn't dream of spending nights with boys. Yeah, that seems about right. Aria has turned him into a big old marshmallow which is really working for me right now.

As Noah and I got out of bed and found our clothes, it didn't take long to realize the house was too quiet. Rivers' voice wasn't sailing up the hallway, convincing Violet to make a massive breakfast and Tully's voice wasn't cursing him out and screaming at him to stop being a lazy prick and to make his own damn breakfast.

Coming out of Noah's room, I see that Tully's door is still closed and there's not even a hint of movement within. Rivers either forgot to set the alarm on her phone or she let it go, opting to spend the day wasting away in bed.

Walking out into the living room and coming through to the kitchen, it was made clear that Rivers wasn't there. Though, my first thought was that he could be in Tully's room with her, but it's a move he wouldn't risk with Noah there which was when I realized that his shoes weren't by the front door and his phone, keys, and wallet which usually sit on the hallway table were gone.

A horn blares in the student parking lot, snapping me back to reality as I finish off what's left of my coffee. "Shit, that wasn't enough," I tell Noah as he glances around the lot, searching for the idiot who's honking their horn. I continue rambling on. "What a strange fucking morning. Is everything going to be ass up today or is that it? I'd really like it if from now on, everything could be normal," I add, shaking my head. "I'm definitely going to need another coffee if I plan on getting through today."

"That bad?" he grumbles as a cringe graces his face.

"Uh huh," I say, studying him closely as Tully's Jeep pulling up beside Noah's Camaro steals both of our attention.

"Shit," I say, looking her over as she climbs out of the Jeep with her massive dark glasses on, clearly trying to deal with a nasty hangover. "I didn't think she'd come today."

"Yeah," he grumbles to himself before an amused chuckle pulls from deep within him. "Neither did I."

I watch her a moment as she walks around her Jeep and collects her things from the passenger side. Everything she does is just a bit slower and when she looks up and gives me a pathetic little smile, a painful twinge cuts through me.

She was still in bed when we left and considering we've only been here for a few minutes, she must have rolled out of bed and gotten straight in the car right after we left. There wouldn't have been time to stop for coffee or get herself breakfast, and considering she's still in the same jeans from last night and her hair hasn't been done, I'd say it's going to be one hell of a bad day for her.

She starts making her way up to the school and it's almost as though she can sense him. Her head whips around and zones in on Rivers over on the other side of the lot. I hadn't even seen him myself and I'm in a much better position to. I don't even think Noah did.

Rivers walks up to the school with his arm thrown over Alyssa's shoulder and I let out a sigh. At least that answers where he disappeared to this morning. I flick back to Tully just in time to see her whole world deflate. I can't see her eyes, but something tells me that seeing them together right now is killing her.

"Fuck," Noah murmurs as his phone chimes in the center console. "She really likes him, doesn't she?" he questions as he releases my hand to grab the phone.

"You've got no idea," I grumble, watching him as he scans over the text with a frown which quickly morphs into a cringe, sending suspicion sailing right through me. "What is it?" I question, quickly glancing up to check on Rivers as a bad feeling settles into my stomach, and sure enough, he's standing still in the middle of the lot, checking his phone.

Fuck. That could only mean one thing; Anton Fucking Mathers.

My world crashes down around me. I hate it when he does this shit. "No," I silently beg, looking up at him and still hoping for the best.

Noah's face crumbles and it absolutely kills me. "I'm sorry, babe. I have to go."

"Don't," I tell him as my heart breaks, hating the type of work he does for the guy. He's so much better than this. "Tell Anton to get fucked. You don't need to be doing this."

"It's not that easy, Henley," he tells me with frustration as Rivers starts jogging this way to kick me out and take my place.

"Of course, it's that fucking easy," I demand, starting to get pissed off. "You two are going to end up in prison for that douchebag. How could you be so stupid to throw your lives away like that?"

"I have to," Noah yells back at me, clenching his jaw to try to reign in his emotions. "You fucking know this. I can't stop. I owe him."

"Because of Lily?" I question. "Don't think you think she'd be fucking ashamed seeing what you do for him?"

Noah slams his hand down on the dash, making me jump. "Don't you ever fucking speak for her again. You didn't know her, you never did. So how the fuck can you sit there pretending you know how she would feel about this?" he roars. "Anton gave her twelve fucking months," he reminds me. "She never would have gotten that without him. I owe him my fucking life."

"But you don't-"

"No," he yells, not even giving me a chance to get my point across. "Get the fuck out, Henley. Go to school."

I look up at him with hurt only to see a fierce determination etched into his face. I grab my bag and reach for my phone before releasing the door. "You're a real fucking disappointment, Noah," I tell him, hoping it cuts just as bad as he cut me.

I push my way out of his car and make sure to slam the door with everything I've got before walking away, fighting to control myself as Rivers jogs past me. "What the fuck's wrong with you?" he questions, not really asking as he continues on to Noah's Camaro.

"I'm not fucking bailing you out when you dickheads get arrested," I throw over my shoulder.

Do not fucking cry. Do not cry.

I get up to my locker and see Tully down the hall and for once I don't actually give a shit. She can come to me if she wants. All I care to do right now is to knock some fucking heads together, maybe draw a little blood too.

I mean, how dare he? Yeah, I maybe took it a little too far suggesting Lily would be ashamed, but that's just common sense, right? What little sister wouldn't hate her big brother getting involved in that bullshit? But he didn't have to yell at me like that.

What have I done? Allowing myself to get this close to a guy? Giving him my heart and allowing him free reign over it. I should have known shit would start going south soon enough. I should reclaim my heart to avoid the inevitable heartbreak, but I don't actually think it's possible. Once you give it away, it's fucking hard getting it back, and I fear Noah is going to hold claim over it for the rest of our lives.

So, if I'm fucking stuck with him, that douche canoe better come up with one hell of an apology, otherwise it's going to be a shit show when he gets back from serving his deranged boss.

Shit. How is it so possible to hate someone while being furiously in love with him at the same time? Damn it. This fucking sucks.

Tully falls into the locker beside mine. "Who are we beating up at lunch?" she questions. "You look like shit."

"Like you're one to talk," I say. "How's your hangover?"

"We're not talking about me."

"Well, we sure as hell aren't talking about me," I tell her, pulling out my books and closing the locker door. I lean back into it and let out a sigh. "How is it possible for your brother to be such a dickhead?"

Tully grins to herself. "I knew it wouldn't take much for you to break, but I sure as hell thought it'd take a bit more than that."

"Can't help it," I tell her, sulking like a little bitch. "I'm so fucking angry with him."

"What did he do now?" she questions.

I shake my head. "Just the usual Anton bullshit," I tell her. "I might have suggested that Lily would be ashamed of him."

Tully sucks in a sharp breath. "Fuck. That wouldn't have gone down well."

115

"It didn't," I agree. "He lost his fucking mind and then kicked me out."

"Damn," she sighs. "You know his head is going to be all sorts of fucked up today."

"Yeah, I know," I tell her, hating that I'm the one who made that happen. "I just…I can't stand him working for a guy like that. I don't want to be visiting him in prison for the rest of our lives."

"Same," she murmurs with a tight smile, looking down at her feet. "Was Rivers going with him?"

"What do you think?" I grumble, knowing she hates it just as much as I do, though she doesn't quite know the reasons behind why Noah does it and he wants it to stay like that despite the feeling I get that she knows more than he thinks. Rivers though, who knows what the hell his reasons are for working for a guy like Anton.

"Damn it," Tully groans as fury shines bright through her green eyes. "Come on, let's get the fuck out of here."

Maybe we shouldn't be together right now. I can just see it now; we're going to end up in shit for doing something reckless and stupid to relieve our anger. Naturally, the dickhead boys will come in and try to rescue us from ourselves and then we'll have no choice but to forgive them. Well, that shit ain't going to happen. Not today.

The bell sounds and I shake my head. "No. Go to homeroom. We'll curse out their asses at lunch, and besides, if I want even the slightest chance of getting this scholarship, I have to be here."

Tully lets out a deep breath which comes out as more of an annoyed huff. "Fine," she says. "But the cursing out is starting now. Keep your phone on you or I'll be forced to come and bombard you in class."

I resist laughing, realizing her threat is real. I wouldn't put it past her to come and sit in my class just to bitch about Rivers, despite a teacher yelling at her the whole time, though, when she realizes that Alyssa is in most of my classes, she'll probably change her mind.

By the time lunch has come around, the battery on my phone is just about gone. When Tully warned me that the cursing out was going to start during homeroom, she fucking meant it.

She blew up my phone like never before while I sat in class watching out the window, waiting to see that familiar white Camaro.

To be honest, I was surprised when it returned twenty minutes ago. I was sure as hell that the two of them would have avoided coming here like the plague. Surely, they must know that they have two very pissed off girls to face.

I walk down to the cafeteria and all I can think about is laying into him with everything I've got, but the second I walk through the big double doors and see those green eyes of his staring back at me, I suddenly don't feel so brave.

He looks hurt. Not the physical kind, but the deep in his soul kind of hurt and I hate that I was the one who put it there. It pulls at my heart strings, but I still can't get past the fact that he took me down the way he did, over fucking Anton Mathers of all people.

Tully is nowhere to be seen and Rivers, well, who the fuck knows? All that matters is that Noah is sitting across the room, staring at me with unease. I'd dare say he's cooled down from this morning. Noah and Rivers probably didn't talk about it, whereas Tully and I have hung on every last detail all day long, only fueling our anger.

I guess I was kind of hoping Noah would storm up to me in some kind of rage and give me a chance to get it all out, but now, I only feel deflated. Being mad at him is hard fucking work.

An arm loops though mine and draws my attention away from Noah. "What do you think you're doing?" Tully demands. "You look like a lost puppy dog who just found her owner. You're not going to cave that easily."

"I wasn't going to cave," I defend, lying like the little bitch that I am.

"Yes, you were," she tells me, pulling me towards the cafeteria line. "You were two seconds away from stripping off butt naked and offering yourself up to him like an all you can eat buffet. Trust me," she continues, "that look in his eye is dangerous. He's still more than ready to lay your ass out."

I roll my eyes before looking back over my shoulder at him. His eyes are still on me but as I take a deeper look, she's right. I was distracted by my overwhelming feelings for him and completely missed the heavy scowl that accompanies the fury behind his eyes.

Noah's got his game face on. He hasn't cooled down at all.

Shit.

What the fuck was I thinking? I was more than ready to waltz over there and start groveling at his feet, apologizing for being such a self-absorbed insensitive bitch, and it wouldn't have gotten me anywhere except made me look weak.

I narrow my eyes on the fucker only to get a wicked smirk in response. "Oh, that fucking rat bastard," I seethe through my teeth, loud enough that I'm sure he hears me; him and everyone else in the room.

Noah pushes to his feet with nothing but a challenge in his eye as he spreads his arms out wide. "Fucking try me, babe."

Red. Fucking red. Every last damn thing I see is red.

It's fucking on.

I get my bitch claws out and start towards him, barging kids out of my way as I go. Noah all but does the same, only the kids near him are smart enough to get out of his way before he does it for them.

"Shit," I hear a familiar voice across the cafeteria, but it's not familiar enough for me to figure out who it belongs to just yet. "Mommy and Daddy are fighting. Better pick a side now before it all goes to hell."

The closer Noah gets, the thinner his glare becomes and it's fucking terrifying, but I know he'll never hurt me. He needs to scream just as much as I do. We're just fucked up enough to let it happen right here in the middle of the cafeteria where the whole fucking world can see.

"No, no, no, no," Tully says, hurrying behind me, trying to grab my arm to hold me back. "Not like this," she begs, but I hardly hear her over the loud thumping in my ears. I mean. She's more than happy for us to behead each other, she just doesn't want it to turn into a fucking showdown.

My hand stings as I pump my fists by my side.

This fucker is about to go down.

No one crosses Henley Bronx, not even Noah himself.

CHAPTER 12

I storm into Noah, my hand already flying through the air. He ducks back and narrowly escapes one hell of a bitch slap. I should have known better. Noah has endured more than his fair share of pissed off woman.

Something flashes in his eyes but it's gone quicker than I can get a read on him. Maybe he's pissed that I'd try to hit him or maybe he's hurt by the thought. "You Fucki-"

He grabs my hand and spins me so quickly that the insult falls from my mouth. His steel grip locks my hands behind my back and before I know it, he's storming through the emergency exit and setting off the fire alarm. Though naturally, he doesn't give a shit, just keeps pushing me in front. "Let me go, you big bastard," I demand, struggling against his grip, only to get nothing but a furious growl from behind me.

He forces me across the school and towards the old art block where the school has practically been deserted. He slams through the door of the photography room and only stops once he's pushed me through to the dark room.

Noah releases his hold on me to lock the door, making me wonder how he even knew there was a lock there. Though this is Noah Cage, he probably brought chicks down here to screw all the time before me.

Noah finishes with the door and I spin to face him, my hand desperate for another attempt at his face. "Fucking do it," he growls, crowding me and getting in my face while knowing exactly what I need to help rid me of this anger.

I don't hesitate. Not for one fucking second.

My hand slaps hard across his heated skin and I'm left fighting for breath as my palm begins to sting. Tears instantly fill my eyes as I'm overwhelmed by my emotions. I just hit the man I love and what's more, he let me do it. This couldn't be normal.

I slam my hand into his hard chest, wondering why the fuck he just allowed me to do that. "You-"

"No," he demands, hitting my hand away.

I'm instantly clouded with guilt, but he's already there, hands on my ass, lifting me and slamming me hard into the wall of the dark room.

A gasp is ripped out of me as Noah's lips crush down on mine, completely swallowing it. He pins me against the wall with his body, freeing his hand to tear my shirt over my head. His lips are hard against mine. It's not pretty. It's desperate, needy, and messy, but hell, there's no way I'm about to stop.

My hands reach around him and scramble for the fabric of his shirt before pulling hard. I rip it over his head before tossing it away and digging my nails back into the skin of his back, holding on for dear life as my man takes it out on my body.

He rids me of my jeans and I climb back up his body as he undoes his own. My legs wrap tightly around his waist as my arm curls around his neck, keeping me in place.

His jeans haven't even hit the ground before he slams into me.

I scream out his name, panting and moaning right along

with him. His fingers dig into my skin and I'm sure as hell it will bruise, but I don't give a shit. I'm sure my nails have probably cut into his skin by now, but it's not like he's stopping me.

He slams into me over and over again, his lips still crushed against mine, right until the end when he helps me find the release we're both desperately searching for.

There's nothing better than angry sex. I don't give a shit what anyone says, I will forever stand by it. Emotions are wild and when you're at breaking point, there's only one way to solve it, you know, considering you're not about to break out into a brawl, of course.

Talking will only go so far and Noah's never really been one for talk. He prefers to show me how he feels and it's always in the best kind of ways.

He pulls out of me but doesn't let me go as he hangs his head on my shoulder, breathing me in as we both catch our breath. His hands curl around my back holding me close to him as he spins us around, putting his back against the wall.

Noah slides down until he's on the ground with me sitting in his lap. "I shouldn't have yelled at you this morning," he murmurs, raising his head until his eyes are piercing right into mine.

I shake my head, agreeing with him. "No, you shouldn't have, but I shouldn't have brought up Lily. That was a low blow."

"You bet your ass, it was," he grumbles, taking a deep breath and slowly releasing it.

I silently watch him, studying the lines of his face, getting lost deep in thought as he watches me right back. "Why'd it hit you so hard?" I ask, treading carefully. "Surely, you must know how she'd feel about it."

He looks down, taking his eyes from mine and unknowingly killing me inside. His hands remain on my waist, his thumbs sailing back and forth over my warm skin. "I know exactly how she'd feel about it," he murmurs, refusing to look up as though he's ashamed of himself, killing me all over again. "She'd fucking hate it. You were right, she'd be ashamed of me."

"Noah," I whisper, holding onto him a little tight, wishing I could somehow take away his pain.

"Lily was too young to know anything about Anton," he continues, "but every fucking time I go to work for him, it's all I can think about, knowing she'd be looking down on me and seeing that. It makes me fucking sick. She'd hate it."

"You can't do this to yourself," I tell him, tipping his chin to force him to look back up at me. "You need to stop."

"As much as I want to, it's not that easy."

"Why not?" I question. "Surely, you must have paid off your debt to him. You've been working for him for years."

"It doesn't work like that," he explains. "When a guy like Anton does you a favor, you're selling your soul to him. He owns me now and there's not a damn thing I can do about it. Having me and Rivers around is far too convenient for him, he'll never let us go. We know the area, we know the people, we don't show fear, and we can just about talk our way out of anything. We're fucking gold mines to him."

"But-"

"No, buts," he says, cutting me off with a tight, apologetic smile. "Trust me, if there was a 'but' we would have gotten out a long time ago."

"So, you actually want out?"

"Of course, I do," he says, leaning in and gently pressing his lips to mine. "You think I like seeing the look on your face every time I have to go do a job? You think I like hiding it from my parents and knowing that Lily would be rolling in her grave if she knew. No way in hell."

I let out a breath and lean forward, resting my forehead against his. "I'm sorry," I tell him. "I didn't mean to hurt you."

"Spitfire," he sighs. "Baby, you didn't. You just reminded me how much I hated myself. I am a disappointment."

"You're not," I tell him. "You're the best person I've ever known. You're so strong and loyal. It's part of the reason I love you so much and it kills me that I said those things to you this morning. You kicked me out of your car and I was so angry, the words just came out. Please, don't be mad at me. I can't take it anymore."

He smiles up at me. "How could I possibly be mad at you?"

"You yelled at me."

"You yelled at me," he fires back.

"Yeah, but…you were being an idiot."

"And you weren't?" he says before letting out a breath. "You hit me."

"You told me to."

"But…before that," he says, referring to the almost slap in the cafeteria.

I let out a broken sigh. "I know. I'm sorry. It's just…you have this ability to infuriate me and don't act as though it wasn't provoked. 'Fucking try me, babe'," I mimic.

"You called me a rat bastard for the whole fucking school to hear. What was I supposed to do? Get down on my hands and knees and grovel for your forgiveness? Show weakness in front of the vultures? Yeah fucking right."

"I guess we put on a bit of a show," I murmur.

"You guess?" he scoffs. "That little performance is going to have them forgetting all about Nate and Jackson's race."

I roll my eyes, realizing he's right. "Who made the mommy and daddy fighting comment?"

Noah scoffs again. "Spencer," he says with a bit of a huff. "Guess the fucker didn't learn his lesson the first and second time."

"Guess not," I grumble, wrapping my arms around his neck. "Are we all good?"

"Yeah, Spitfire. I'm sorry I yelled at you. I think I was surprised to hear you say that about Lily when it's only ever something that's been inside my head. No one's ever said something to me like that before."

"Well, you've never really let anyone close enough to know you before."

"And I just had to pick the one strong enough to put me in my place."

"Damn straight, you did," I laugh before climbing off his lap and searching around for my clothes. "Come on," I tell him. "I need to eat before our lunch break is over and I think we need to show all the vultures that nothing can tear us apart, not even ourselves."

"Nah," he says, reaching for me. "Let's just stay here."

I smirk down at him. "Tell me, Noah. How did you know there was a lock on this door? Have you been in here before?"

"Oh, shit," he says, jumping to his feet and grabbing his clothes. "Lunch is nearly over and you need to eat. Let's not waste any time."

"Yeah, that's what I thought," I laugh as we get ourselves dressed.

It doesn't take long before we're walking back to the cafeteria, hand in hand. "So, correct me if I'm wrong here, but it sort of looked like Tullz was about ready to kill me too."

"Yeah," I laugh.

"What?" he questions. "Why? What the fuck did I do to her?"

I shrug my shoulders. "Girl Code."

"Are you serious? My own sister turned her back on me."

"Hey," I defend. "You're not the one who's listened to her ranting about how much she hates Rivers right now. She owed me."

He lets out a sigh. "What's going on with them, anyway?" he questions. "One minute they're hot, the next cold. They've always had this thing between them, but it's never been this bad. I swear, it's almost as though Tully is about to shred him to pieces."

I look away as he thinks it over. "Shit," he sighs.

"What?"

"She made a move, didn't she? And he turned her down. That's the only thing that could make sense. Fuck. No wonder she's hating on him so much." I let out a breath as he looks down at me. "But you already knew that, didn't you?"

"Yeah," I sigh, hating that I'm not telling him the whole truth right now. "He turned her down and it tore her apart. You know, I think they're in love with each other."

Noah scoffs. "Yeah, right," he laughs. "They like each other, sure, but they're not in love."

"You sure about that?"

I smile as he looks back down at me, now not so sure of himself. "Are you sure about it?"

I nod. "Think so."

"Ok, so if that was the case, why the fuck would he turn her down? Not because of me?"

"I mean, I guess you're part of the reason. He doesn't want to be disrespectful to you, but more than that, he doesn't think he's good enough for her."

"Shit, well, no fucker is good enough for her," he tells me, "but...fuck. I don't know. I don't like the idea of her with anyone."

"Of course, you don't. You're her brother. That's how you're supposed to feel, but one day, she's going to be with someone whether or not you approve of him."

"Stop," he says. "You're totally killing my vibe, right now."

I shrug my shoulders and laugh. "I'm just saying it like it is. She'll find some guy, get married and have kids. But when you think of her like that, wouldn't you prefer the guy to be Rivers, knowing how much he cares about her? He's so loyal, just like you. He'd never let her get hurt."

"It'll never happen," he tells me. "Even if they dated for a short while. They're both too stubborn. They'd drive each other insane."

"You don't think we're both too stubborn?"

"Yep," he grins. "And you do drive me insane."

"Yet somehow we're making it work."

His mouth snaps shut and I grin to myself. Point proven. I think that'll give him a little something to think about.

We keep making our way back to the cafeteria when we pass the science classrooms. I pull back on Noah's hand, seeing Mr. Carver eating his lunch at his desk rather than the staff room like most of the teachers do. I come to a stop in his doorway and knock gently to get his attention. "Sorry to disturb you," I say.

"No, no," he says, quickly wiping his mouth and welcoming us into his classroom. "What's going on? How can I help you?"

"I just wanted to stop by and let you know that I've decided to go for the scholarship."

His eyes widen in surprise as though he had expected me to reject it. "Really? That's great news. Can I ask what changed your mind?"

"Well, apart from all my excuses, which all still stand by the way, a few people made me realize that I'd be a fool if I didn't even try. I mean it's better to have tried than to give up."

"Indeed, it is," Carver says as his eyes cut across to Noah, making it clear he knows who I mean by a 'few people'. "Well, it's good to see that a 'few people' around you seem to have their heads screwed on correctly and can lead you in the right direction."

"Gee, thanks," I grumble, loving that out of all the teachers at Haven Falls Private, it's nice to see that at least one of them actually gives a shit.

"No, problem," he tells me. "I'll arrange a meeting with your other teachers and we'll put together a plan to see if we can get your grades up in your other classes. You realize it's not going to be easy, right? You're going to have to work your butt off to prove to the administration board at Broken Hill University that you belong there."

"Yep, I know."

"You really mean it? Don't waste my time if you don't plan on putting in the effort. I'd really like to see you succeed, Henley."

"I mean it," I tell him with a definite nod.

"Excellent," he says. "Then get that application form filled out and I'll write you a recommendation."

I give him a grateful smile before a cringe takes over. "About the application form," I say, resisting scowling back at Noah. "Could I get another one?"

"Why?" he asks, narrowing his eyes on me. "You didn't burn the old one the second you walked out of my class, did you?"

"I'm not going to lie," I tell him. "The thought did cross my mind, but someone got a little too confident and started filling it out for me. Completely did it all wrong."

"Ok," he laughs, walking back over to his desk and rifling through his bottom drawer. "That I can deal with." A moment later, he pulls out a brand new application form and hands it over. "Maybe fill it out yourself, this time."

"I will," I smile. "I'll let you get back to your lunch."

"Thanks," he says as we turn and start heading for the door. "Oh, and Henley," he calls behind us, "come prepared to class this afternoon. We've got a pretty exciting experiment."

Yes. I resist fist pumping the sky. My day just got that much better.

We walk out and I close the door behind me, feeling all kinds of happy until the doormat next to me insists on opening his mouth. "Is that guy deranged?" he grunts. "What kind of idiot calls an experiment exciting?"

Ugh. Stupid boys. They just don't get it.

CHAPTER 13

"So, what the hell do we do now if we can't go to the races on a Friday night?" I ask Noah as we sit out front of his home, watching the cars go by.

Noah shrugs his shoulders and scrunches up his face. "I don't fucking know," he grumbles before glancing away, trying to hide the fact that the races being shut down really bothers him. The races were something he looked forward to, a place to go where he could let loose and kick people's asses with nothing but practiced ease.

And now it's all gone and there's nowhere for him to release that need within to feel the tires spinning beneath him, to feel the engine rumble and being pushed to its max, to feel the adrenaline of the race and the crowd chanting his name. All freaking gone.

"We could always go and find some sorry loser to drag race," I suggest, though I hope he knows I'm joking to try to cheer him up. There's no way I'd let him drag race. But then, I guess if it's something he actually wanted to do, we'd already be out there searching for an opponent despite everyone's better judgment.

Noah's not exactly the type to not do something because someone else told him not to. He does what he wants to do and I love that attitude about him, I just worry it's going to get him into trouble one day.

"Nah," he says shrugging off the suggestion as though it had a bit of merit. "It'd be good, but drag racing is too much effort. We have to shut down the streets and that brings too much attention. Besides, the Camaro is too loud and too easily recognized for that shit."

My eyes flick over to the car in question as Tully scoffs from inside. "You could take your girl out on a date like a regular fucking dude," she yells through the open door.

I choke back a laugh as Noah's eyes shoot to mine. "What the hell are you laughing at?"

"It's just…I don't think we've ever actually been on a date."

"What?" he grunts. "Of course we have."

"Name one time."

Tully calls out once again. "Bet you fifty bucks he can't."

"I'm not taking that bet," I shoot back. "I already know he can't."

"Shut up," Noah scolds. "I'm trying to think."

"Geez, I'm so glad all our dates are so memorable to you," I smirk as a black Firebird pulls up, making Noah sit up a little straighter as he watches the newcomer.

"Who the fuck is this?" he murmurs beside me.

We watch the car for a moment before the door opens and Rivers' head shoots out the driver's side. "You fucking like it?" he calls across the yard as the passenger's side door opens too. "I got a new fucking car."

Noah gets up beside me and walks towards Rivers' new car as Alyssa appears from the passenger side. Shit. Why did he have to bring her here of all places? This is our sacred place. No one in, no one out. I learned that the hard way and here he is walking in with this strange girl. It's bad enough that I'm going to have to pretend to be nice to her considering it looks as though Rivers wants to date her.

I walk forward, pleased that Tully is still inside for now, but it won't be long before she comes out to see what all the fuss is about.

"What the fuck is this piece of shit?" Noah laughs, punching Rivers in the arm.

"Fuck off," Rivers says. "It ain't no piece of shit. It's a fucking gem. She just needs a little work," he nods his head towards the Camaro. "Now, that's a piece of shit."

"Hey, now," I cut in as Alyssa walks around to join us, giving us a nervous smile. "That Camaro is no piece of shit."

Noah walks around the car, doing the usual guy inspection thing as Rivers stands back proudly. "I spoke to Nate over in Broken Hill. He's going to work on her. Get her up to scratch."

"Dude," Noah grumbles. "I doubt you could afford Nate. He's working on multi-million dollar cars. He's not going to do this kind of shit."

"Yeah, but he's got a soft spot for bringing race cars back from the dead."

"True," Noah says, getting back to his inspection, ducking his head in through the driver's door and popping the hood.

Rivers continues watching proudly as he nudges me with his elbow. "What's going on?" he asks, keeping a close eye on Noah's reactions to his car.

Tully shouts through the door once again, clearly not realizing that there's a guest, otherwise, she'd probably be storming out the door in a furious rage. "Noahsaurus is trying to remember if he's ever taken Henley on a date."

"Awwww, shit," Rivers groans, looking to me. "This isn't going to end well." I shake my head, completely agreeing with him as Noah smirks to himself.

Noah's head suddenly shoots up, wide-eyed as he looks to me. "I got it," he shouts proudly. "There was that time we went to that Italian restaurant across from the gas station. You ordered some pasta bullshit."

I shake my head again. "Bum, bum," I say, giving him a thumbs down and impersonating a buzzer as Alyssa chuckles to herself. "I don't know who the fuck you went to an Italian restaurant with, but it sure as hell wasn't me."

"Oh, shit," Rivers murmurs to himself.

"Bullshit," Noah says. "I remember it."

"Nah, man," Rivers laughs. "That was Monica. You took her there because she wasn't putting out and you were hoping to…you know."

"Fuck," Noah cringes, looking to me with a guilty as shit expression before a wide smile pulls over his lips. He strides towards me and crashes down into me, sending us both down to the ground and making me squeal out like a little bitch before he nuzzles his face into my neck. "Sorry, babe," he says with a chuckle, drawing the words out. "How do you feel about Italian tonight?"

I laugh as I try to push him off me but the fucker isn't budging. "You're so fucking lucky I'm in a good mood, Noahsaurus."

"Do you really have to call me that?" he grunts, pulling his head up.

"Considering you just thought your date with Monica was with me, you're lucky that's all I'm calling you."

"She's got a point, man," Rivers laughs. "Quit while you're behind."

"Fine," he groans. "You can call me anything you want."

"Damn fucking straight, I can."

Noah rolls his eyes as Tully comes striding out of the house with a slice of last night's pizza before stopping mid step, taking in Alyssa standing beside Rivers. "What the fuck is this?" she demands, pizza completely forgotten.

As if forgetting Alyssa standing right beside him, Rivers' eyes trail down her body, taking in the tight black dress and heels. "Where the hell do you think you're going dressed like that?" Rivers sputters making Alyssa stand a little taller, though I don't know if that's because she's trying to make herself seen or if she finally sees the threat from Tully.

Tully narrows her eyes on him while somehow managing to appear as though their very presence doesn't affect her. "It's Friday night," she reminds him. "I have my date with Rocko tonight."

"Rocko Stevenson?" Alyssa says, sucking in a breath as though she's impressed with Tully's efforts. She instantly gets ignored.

Noah scrambles off me as Rivers steps forward. "No fucking way."

Noah cuts him off. "I thought we sorted this shit already."

"Wait," Alyssa cuts in, making all eyes turn her way. "If you're going on a date with Rocko, why are you eating now?"

Rivers' eyes slice to Tully with the smallest seed of hope that she isn't going on a date after all, but Tully has been talking about this date for days. She's not about to back out of it, especially now that she's seen Rivers with Alyssa. Besides, isn't it a well known fact that girls eat before their date so they don't look like the slob that they actually are in front of a new guy?

"No, we didn't sort this" Tully says slowly, turning back to her brother and completely disregarding anything that comes from Alyssa's mouth. "You guys spoke at me while I failed to listen. You see, what you guys fail to do is realize that I no longer give a shit. I'm a grown ass woman and I can make my own decisions about who I date, so," she adds, pointedly looking at Rivers, "unless you have a better idea of who should be taking me out tonight, then I subtly suggest you both mind your own fucking business. Besides," she adds, "it looks as though you already have someone else you should be focusing on tonight."

Rivers grinds his teeth as Noah scowls. "I don't like it."

"I never asked you too."

"Tullz," Rivers sighs. "Come on. Don't go out with him. Date someone else if you have to, just not him."

"You're too late, Rivers. I'm going whether you like it or not," she tells him before turning on her heel and heading back inside.

Both the boys look to me. "What?" I grunt, holding up both hands. "There's nothing I can do about it. I've already tried. Besides, she's right. She's eighteen and more than capable of making her own decisions. If she wants to go on a date with the guy, then so be it. She'll probably come home tonight and realize what a turd he is and never go on one again."

"I can still hear you," Tully yells from inside.

"I don't care," I say, getting back to my rant. "Point is that she needs to come to the decision on her own, not have two overbearing assholes in her face demanding she not go. Besides," I say, turning solely on Rivers before waving my hand over Alyssa, not giving a shit if I'm about to offend her. "You're making it fucking worse. There might have been a chance that Tully changed her mind on her own, but not now."

With that, I turn and make my way inside as Alyssa gapes behind me.

"Shit," Rivers murmurs as I make my way back towards the house.

"Fuck, man," Noah grumbles. "Why'd you have to bring her here?"

"What's the fucking problem?" Rivers snaps. "I used to bring chicks here all the time. She never had a problem with it before."

"Yeah, but...things are different now."

I don't hear Rivers' response as I disappear inside.

The second I step over the threshold and the door is firmly sealed shut behind me, Tully instantly starts fuming while repeatedly trying to insert her earrings, only her anger makes it impossible. "Can you fucking believe him?" she seethes. "How dare he bring that tramp here?"

I cringe. This isn't exactly a conversation I want to be involved in. She should be screaming at Rivers, not me, but I guess that's the role I take on as her best friend. "I, well, maybe he was too excited about the car and didn't think about what he was doing," I suggest, hoping that's somewhat helpful.

"Nice try, but no," she grunts. "Rivers is the most calculated person you'll ever meet. He doesn't take a shit without thinking about it first. There's no way he just got excited and drove straight here with her."

Damn, if she knew about the shit he took on the side of the road a few weeks ago, she'd have no choice but to change her argument on the whole 'calculated' thing, but then, he is the guy who convinced me to make a game plan when taking down Monica rather than bursting in with my claws ready. I let out a sigh. "I don't know, Tully," I say, terrified of saying the wrong thing and making it worse. "I can't tell you what was going through his head."

"I fucking can," she all but yells across the room before storming off to her room with me following behind. "He's purposefully trying to hurt me," she insists, throwing herself in front of her mirror to put her earrings in. "I've been talking about Rocko and whoring around, and now he's going to do the same just to give me the middle finger."

"Maybe he actually likes her," I suggest.

Cringe.

"Likes her or likes the fact that she has a little, willing, pink pussy to sink into each night?" she scoffs with an attitude I've never quite seen from her before, telling me just how much this is bothering her.

This isn't going anywhere good.

She perks up a little and looks at me through the mirror. "Get out there and scare her off," she tells me. "I don't want her barging her way into our lives."

I shake my head. "I don't either, but I can't do it. Rivers

is my friend too and if he actually likes her, then he deserves a chance to be happy too."

"You're such a fucking pushover now that you're in love," she mumbles. "I liked you better when you had that big fucking wall up. Nobody could even get near you then. Especially chicks like that."

I shrug my shoulders. "Sorry for giving a shit," I laugh. "And for the record, you guys got close and I still haven't worked out how to get rid of you."

"Keep letting Alyssa hang out and you won't have an issue getting rid of me."

"You know, Rivers will come around one day," I tell her. "He just needs to fuck everything up first."

She lets out a frustrated groan before walking over to her makeup box and finding a lip gloss. "He already did fuck everything up and then I fucked it all up some more by sleeping with Spencer again. There's no going back for us. We're too far gone which is why I'm trying so hard to move on. I can't keep thinking about him like this all the time. It's going to kill me. I have to move on."

I move across her room and drop down onto her bed. "Are you sure, though?" I question, giving her a tight smile. "Are you sure you don't want to give it one last shot with him? Maybe wait a few months. He might just need a little time to cool down. You never know."

"But I do know," she says with a heartbreaking sigh. "I've known him since we were eleven. It's not something he's about to budge on. I'll be waiting years for him to come around and by then, he might be a different guy. A couple of years can change someone."

"But would that change really matter if you're in love with him? He'll still be the same person you've always known."

"I don't know," she says, shrugging her shoulders. "I just want to move on and forget about him."

Tully drops down on her bed beside me and I instantly wrap my arms around her. "It'll be ok," I tell her. "If forgetting about him is what you really want, then that's what we'll do. You can have your date with Rocko tonight and hopefully, he'll rock your world and you'll fall madly in love with the guy, despite everyone else's opinion of him. Then tomorrow night, we can find a party and drink way too much."

She pouts out her bottom lip. "That sounds really, really good."

Tully's phone goes off on her bedside table and I dive for it as she tries to grab it. "Is that him?" I demand, pulling the phone out of her reach.

"Give it back," she yells as I swipe to unlock the screen, but she doesn't put up enough of a fight, telling me she actually doesn't give a shit if I read her text. I look down at the screen before waggling my eyebrows at her with a shit eating grin. "It's from Rocko," I tease.

"Duh," she says, rolling her eyes. "Who else would be texting?"

"Oh, considering the number of guys you've been leading on these past few weeks, I could think of a whole list of people who'd be looking for you on a Friday night."

"Shut up," she laughs. "What does his text say?"

I look down and read it out loud for her.

Rocko – Hey, babe. I'm just leaving my place. Be there in 10.

Tully's eyes widen. "Shit. This is really happening." She stands up and looks herself over in the mirror. "Do I look ok? Is it too slutty? I'm not sure where he's taking me."

"You look amazing," I tell her. "Just take a coat in case it's somewhere classy, though I seriously doubt it. This is Rocko we're talking about. He's probably taking you to McDonald's, so really, you're probably extremely overdressed."

"Damn it," she scolds, looking at me in the mirror again. "You're making me nervous."

"No," I laugh. "You're making you nervous, and really,

there's nothing to be nervous about. You're hot, you look incredible, and you're a hilarious conversationalist. He'll love you. Just keep your legs closed, but if you really must spread 'em, remember to use protection. He most likely has crabs."

A pair of pants flies through the air and smacks me in the face. "I'm not a whore like you. I'm not about to give it up on the first date."

"Uh huh," I say with a grin. "Liar."

The next ten minutes are the longest minutes of my life. After four minutes passed, she started looking out the window. I'd catch her quickly peeking every thirty seconds or so until the familiar car from next door pulled up on the curb.

Tully practically ran outside, grabbing her phone, coat, and bag on the way, desperate to not give Rivers and Noah a chance to interrogate him.

I close the door behind me and find myself scowling at Alyssa's back as I walk towards them. Tully meets Rocko at his car and he insists on getting out and saying 'hey' despite Tully's objections.

Out of respect for his sister, Noah walks forward and shakes his hand, though I don't doubt he had one hell of a tight grip. I hang back and Rocko offers me an awkward smile which I have to admit is better than his usual scowl. Rivers though, he storms straight up to him, barges Noah out of the way and slams Rocko against his own car. "You fucking hurt her and I'll end you."

"Woah," Rocko says, holding his hands up in surrender. "Calm the fuck down, man. We're just going for dinner." Rivers doesn't seem to accept that answer and Rocko turns to Noah. "Yo, could you do something about your boy? He's frothing at the mouth."

Noah steps back. "Sorry, man. Not my business," he tells him. "And honestly, if you can't handle Rivers then you're not good enough to be taking my sister out."

"Suit yourself," Rocko says before making his move. He

goes to deliver a devastating uppercut, but no one can beat Rivers when it comes to fighting dirty.

"Stop," Tully demands, rushing around the car before Rivers can do any damage. Noah flinches, not wanting his sister to get hurt, but Rivers would rather die than allow that to happen. Rocko though, he's probably more concerned about his ego than keeping Tully safe.

Tully grabs Rivers by the shirt and pulls hard, wedging him away from Rocko before sliding herself between them, keeping her eyes on Rivers. "Back off," she demands in a low whisper. "You had your fucking shot. It's not my fault you fucked it up, now let me move on."

Rivers eyes stay locked on Tully's for a long pause before he finally sees something that has him pushing away. "Whatever," he says, walking to his car and indicating to Alyssa to hurry up. "Don't come crying to me when he fucks you over."

"Wouldn't dream of it," she yells back at him.

And just like that, everyone is gone, leaving me and Noah standing alone, wondering what the fuck just went down.

I reach for Noah's hand and lace my fingers through his. He tugs on my hand and my body falls into his as he wraps his arms around me. "Our pack doesn't feel like much of a pack lately," I murmur into his chest. "Everything is falling apart."

"I know," he tells me, running his hand up and down my back. "Everything is fucked up."

"Do you think they'll ever get past this?"

I feel him shrug his shoulders and listen as he lets out a deep breath. "I don't know. We'll always function as a pack," he says. "That will always come first, but when it comes to the way we gel as a group, I don't know. If things get much worse between them, I don't think there will be a way back."

"That was what I was afraid of."

"Me too, Spitfire. Me too."

CHAPTER 14

"Henley," dad yells loudly through the house at the crack of dawn that it startles me from a peaceful sleep. "Answer the damn door."

My eyes blink open to find nothing but darkness. What the hell is he talking about?

A heavy fist slams against the front door in quick succession and my body goes ridged in bed. The last time someone came knocking in the middle of the night, I got the shock of my life.

"Henley," dad yells. "If that boyfriend of yours doesn't quit banging on my door in the next two seconds, I'm going to introduce him to my shotgun."

Shit. It's Noah?

"Spitfire," Noah's singsong voice comes blaring through the walls. "Get that ass of yours out of bed and open this damn door already."

"It's Noah," Aria screeches from her bed. "I'll get it."

Dad's booming voice is nearly enough to wake the dead. "Aria. Don't even think about getting out of bed. There's no

140

way you're getting up this early, go back to sleep. Squish, hurry it up."

Oh dear.

I scramble out of bed and grab the blanket before wrapping it around me and heading down the hallway. Noah raps on the door again and I get to it just in time before he yells out again.

I hurry to pull the deadbolt free and unlock the door before pulling it open to find him more awake than what's socially acceptable, standing here in all his tatted up glory, and smirking at me as though I'm not going to like what I'm about to hear. "What the hell do you think you're doing?" I demand, grabbing the phone in his hand and checking the time. "Noah," I growl. "It's barely even four in the morning. Get lost."

I all but throw the phone back at him and go to slam the door. "Nuh uh," he says, jamming his foot in the door. "Go pack a bag. We're going camping."

I laugh in his face but my howling is quickly interrupted by a yawn that completely takes over me. "Are you insane? The only thing I'm doing is going back to bed. So, you can either come with me and risk my dad trying to murder you, or you can come back in a few hours when the sun has had a chance to actually shine."

Noah shakes his head and gives me an 'I really don't give a shit what you want' smile. "As tempting as going to bed with you right now sounds, you have about two minutes to pack your bag."

"What the hell are you talking about?" I groan.

Noah tsk's me. "Don't keep them waiting," he warns. "You know how they get when they're tired and cranky."

"Huh?"

Noah steps back out of the doorway and I take in his car on the curb to find Tully and Rivers in the back seat of his Camaro, both scowling and certainly not impressed to be there. "You have about three seconds to explain to me what's going on before I lose my fucking mind."

"You wanted our pack back together and that's what we're doing." I raise a brow, waiting for him to continue. "We're going on a road trip and spending the night around a fire, hoping to talk through all our shit and get back on track. I can't deal with their pissy attitudes anymore, so we're forcing them to put it to rest, and if having a few drinks and spending the night in the woods is going to do that, then you bet your ass that's how we're spending our weekend."

"In the woods?"

"You now have one minute to pack your back."

"For fuck's sake, Henley," dad yells. "Get some clothes and get the hell out of here so I can get back to sleep. You know he ain't going to leave without you."

Well, I guess that answers that then.

I look up at Noah before letting out a heavy sigh. "Can you help me? I don't know what to pack. I've never been camping."

"Well, shit, Spitfire," Noah says, stepping through the door. "You're going to have the best fucking time. I bought marshmallows just for you."

"Aren't you sweet," I grumble, dropping the blanket as I step back into my bedroom.

Noah's hand instantly finds my ass as I stand before him in nothing but a pair of purple lace, Brazilian undies, and his old shirt. "Fuck, you look good," he grumbles lowly so no one else in the house can hear.

"Don't even think about it," I warn, slapping his hand away. "You don't get this when you wake me up at four in the morning demanding I go camping. Are you nuts?" I ask, turning to my closet and searching out a bag. "I mean, did you really have to bang on the door until you woke me up? What's wrong with texting or calling? Maybe then hit my bedroom window. Not the front fucking door."

"First off," he says, reaching over the top of my head to grab the bag at the top of my closet. "Shut the fuck up. I did do all that. If you bothered to look at your phone, you'll find about twenty missed calls and texts from me, hell, even a few from Tully and Rivers. After you so miserably failed to wake with that, I tried tapping at your window but it was locked. I even scratched a tree branch across it hoping that if I couldn't wake you the normal way, I could scare you awake, but noooo, that shit didn't work either. Though, that's something we need to discuss. I really need to get you some kind of security system for here, maybe even a big ass dog."

"You're an idiot," I tell him, grabbing a handful of clothes and jamming them into the bag that he holds open for me.

"No," he shoots back. "You're the idiot. Now, hurry it up. We've got a long drive."

"How long?"

"None of your goddamn business," he tells me before grabbing a pair of undies and tossing them right out of the bag. "Trust me," he tells me, "you won't be needing them."

I narrow my eyes and put the undies right back in again.

"Geez, you're really not a morning person, are you?"

"Nope," I grumble, "and the fact that you are is seriously making me reconsider my choices."

"Don't be so dramatic," he says, ruffling my hair and pissing me off just a little bit more. "Get yourself dressed. I'll finish packing your things."

I let out a huff but do as he asks. I look at my choices. Sweatpants or jeans? If I'm going to be stuck in a car for a good portion of the day, then I'm going to have to go with the sweatpants.

I grab a pair and slide them up my legs before ripping off Noah's old shirt and putting on a bra while he takes a sneaky peek. I put the shirt straight back on again and tie the bottom in a knot before rolling up the sleeves a few times and looking as cute as a fucking button.

I throw my hair up in a bun, grab my phone off the charger and slide it into my pocket before grabbing some cash for the inevitable gas station stops along the way.

"Why'd you have to choose camping?" I ask as Noah grabs the blanket from the floor and folds up it.

"Because it's too hard for either of them to escape," he grins as though he has it all worked out. "We'll be too far away for them to walk anywhere, it's my car so neither of them can take off without leaving the rest of us stranded, and in the middle of the woods, they have no choice but to either sulk in a tent or talk to one another. It's a foolproof plan."

"Yeah," I scoff. "Unless they decide to sulk in their tents."

"They won't."

"How do you know that?"

A devilish grin takes over his handsome face. "Because neither of them can resist a good fight."

I look up at him as I let out a low breath. "It's going to be a big day, huh?"

He nods as he pulls me into his arms and presses a kiss to my forehead. "You can sleep in the car."

"Yeah, right," I grumble under my breath, making him chuckle as I step out of his arms. I walk out the door and head for the bathroom to pee and brush my teeth, realizing I probably won't get another chance.

The last time the four of us went anywhere and someone fell asleep, it was like a prank war unleashed upon us. Noah slammed on the brakes, screaming 'brake test' as a whole frozen slushie 'accidentally' got poured all over Tully. She will never sleep in a car with those boys again and I don't doubt she's waiting for her chance at payback.

"Meet me at the car," Noah says through the bathroom door as I finish getting myself ready.

"K," I grumble back, wishing this was all some kind of strange dream. Don't get me wrong, I love what Noah is doing and trying to accomplish here, but camping? Really? Anything but camping. I'm not exactly one to spend my night slapping away mosquitoes and sleeping on the hard, cold ground. I guess the only positive is that I'll get to spend the night, alone in a tent with Noah.

I walk into the kitchen and scrawl out a note for dad, reminding him what's going on as sure as hell, he'll forget, and I don't want him worrying about me more than he already does.

Scanning the cupboard, I grab a packet of potato chips and a box of fruit bars to help us get through to the first gas station, not knowing if those idiots bothered to think about food. Though, I seriously doubt it. If Tully had any warning this was going on, she would have come and found me last night and we would have escaped before it was too late.

Rivers though, he would have just gone with the flow as long as someone else was organizing it.

I make my way out to the car and find Noah has stuffed not only my blanket, but my pillow as well into the front seat. He wasn't kidding that he'll let me sleep in the car, but I'm not risking it. No way in hell.

But that's not all I find in the car. Tully and Rivers are not just sitting in the backseat, they're each facing a window, pointedly looking anywhere but at the other.

"Take your time," Tully murmurs to herself as I get in the car, pulling out my phone to drop it into the center console to find there's already a coffee here waiting for me. My heart swirls, knowing it was Noah who would have thought of it.

"I wouldn't have had to take my time if someone thought of giving me a little heads up," I grumble right back at her as another yawn rips through me.

She kicks the back of the seat. "I did give you a heads up. It's not my fault you're a heavy as fuck sleeper."

I roll my eyes then sit up a little straighter as a light switches on inside Rocko's house next door. I spin around to face Tully. "No, no way. You didn't invite Rocko, did you?"

Rivers' head whips around to Tully before shooting straight back out the window, searching out Rocko's place. "Fuck off. You better not have," he growls. "If that fucker is coming, then Alyssa is coming."

"Shut the fuck up," Tully seethes at him. "I didn't invite him, and for the record, if that slut is coming, then I'm out."

"Yeah," Rivers scoffs. "Because she's the slut here."

Tully's hand whips across the backseat until it's smacking Rivers in the chest. "Excuse me?" she demands. "What did you just call me?"

"You heard me."

Fuck me. This is going to be a really long day. I better grab some painkillers before we go because by the end of this road trip, I'm going to need them.

"Will you two knock it off?" Noah snaps, dropping down into the driver's seat and starting the engine.

"Dude, this isn't a fucking good idea," Rivers says, sounding as though this isn't the first time he's said it this morning.

"Why?" Noah snaps back at him with a raised brow. "Because you have a fucking hard time keeping your hands off my sister?"

Tully's mouth drops open as Rivers' eyes practically bulge out of their sockets. "Nah, man," he rushes out. "No fucking problem there."

"Good," Noah grunts as Tully scowls across at Rivers. "We've got a long fucking trip and I'm not listening to you two fuckheads arguing the whole way. And for the record, none of your loser add ons are welcome. So, shut the fuck up and pretend like you give a shit."

Their eyes sail back out their windows as the argument promptly dies.

Well, that shut 'em up.

I beam at Noah. "And that's why I keep you around."

A cheesy grin cuts across his face as he reaches over and takes my hand, placing it on the gear stick with his sitting firmly on top, more than ready to get this trip over and done with.

"Fuck, can we stop?" Tully whines from the backseat five

hours later. "I need to pee."

"Seriously?" Rivers groans. "We've already stopped for your weak ass bladder three times. You couldn't possibly need to pee again."

"Well, if dickhead in the front didn't wake me up so early, I wouldn't have just finished my third coffee. Besides," she adds with a scoff. "Don't act as though you haven't peed off the side of the road every time we stopped."

"Shit," Noah groans cutting off whatever Rivers was bound to snap back at her with as he looks up in the rearview mirror, probably to scold her. "Have you seriously drunk three coffees? I only bought extra large ones."

"Tell me about it," she says with a desperate little groan. "And my bladder is only big enough to hold one of them. So, hurry up and find another gas station."

Rivers chuckles. "Have you been paying attention at all?" he grins, loving a chance to shut her down. "There's no more gas stations for miles. If you gotta pee, it's gotta be on the side of the road."

"Fuck, no," she screeches, searching out Noah's eyes in the mirror. "Is he fucking with me?"

"Nope, sorry, Tullz," Noah responds. "You have three options. You can either squat out by some prickly ass weeds, try to shoot it into a cup, or hold it. What's it going to be?"

"You're a fucking jerk," she snaps as I press my hand over my mouth, desperately trying to hold in a laugh as to not anger the beast behind me. A resigned sigh comes sailing out of her. "Pull over," she instructs Noah as Rivers howls with laughter.

Noah's Camaro comes to a stop and Tully practically dives out of the car. She quickly looks around and it doesn't take long to realize that there are no trees to hide behind, no divots in the land, no bushes, literally nowhere for her to hide. "Shit," she groans. "You big bastards better turn the fuck around. If I catch either of you looking, I'm going to make the next twenty four hours a living hell for you."

And this time, they know she means every single word of it.

They instantly turn around and I dive back into the car. "Wait," I call out before grabbing a handful of tissues. "You don't want to leave without these."

Tully rolls her eyes but grabs them before taking off. Shrugging my shoulders, I grab a few more and take off with her. You know, I don't want to waste an opportunity.

Tully goes off to the left and I head right.

I find a nice little patch of grass and try to work out how to do this. Do I just pull my pants down or take them off completely? I don't want to risk peeing all over them. I guess that answers my question. I whip my pants and undies right off, not really giving a shit if the boys turn around. I mean, that's their loss, not mine.

I squat down in the grass and try to convince myself to let it go, but the awkwardness of it all makes it a little hard, especially when I look up and find Noah's eyes on me with one hell of a massive smirk on his face. "Do you need me to sing a song or something?" he calls.

I give him a thumbs up. "All good," I yell back, grinning to myself when I look further to notice Rivers standing across the other side of the road with his back to us, so very clearly peeing once again.

Geez, the joys of road trips.

I get myself sorted out, pleased as hell I thought of the tissues. I pull my clothes back on and start heading back to the Camaro, feeling as though I've just accomplished something. I mean, not many girls could proudly say they squatted on the side of the road, right? Me, though. I'm a fucking champion. Taking a shit like Rivers had to do after being locked up...now, that might be taking it a little too far.

We get back in the car and once everyone is happy, Noah takes off, and hopefully, our next stop will be the final one.

Ten minutes later, we drive past a gas station while Noah and Rivers howl like fucking hyenas.

CHAPTER 15

Noah slams on the brakes, jolting us all forward in our seats. I throw my hands up, bracing myself against the dashboard while feeling Tully slam into the back of my chair with a loud 'Oomph.'

"What the fuck, man?" Rivers grunts, grabbing onto Tully, trying to pull her back, and only just having enough time to throw his other hand up to save himself from smashing into the back of Noah's seat.

"Hold on," Noah calls, pulling to the side of the road before glancing in his mirrors and performing a massive turn across the deserted highway until we're heading back the other way. "I think I saw something."

"Like what?" I grumble.

"Shut up, I'm looking," Noah says as he leans forward in his seat and squints at everything before him as if that could somehow make him see better. I mean, why do people do this? Squinting is probably making it worse. It's the same as when people turn down the music to help them see street signs or the numbers on mailboxes better. Freaking ridiculous.

"Looking for what?" Tully groans, rubbing the side of her face and unintentionally prompting Rivers to reach out and gently run his fingers over the red mark that's appearing there. She flinches back from his touch and not a second later, hurt flashes in both their eyes.

"You'll see," Noah promises before a huge, face splitting grin takes over his face. "I fucking knew it," he cheers, pointing out the windshield. "Look at that."

Noah brings his Camaro to a stop in the middle of the highway, forcing me to whip my head around and double check that there are no cars sitting on our six. Satisfied that the highway is completely deserted, I give in and play along with whatever Noah has deemed to be the most exciting part of our trip so far.

Noah's eyes settle on me as I look out the windshield and try to work out what's caught his attention. It doesn't take long for a smile to spread wide across my face as I take in the old street sign that's well on its way to falling down, pointing towards an overgrown, forgotten, dirt road. "It's Henley Road," I beam. "It's my road."

"Sure fucking is, Spitfire," Noah murmurs, proud as fuck of himself.

I can practically hear Rivers rolling his eyes in the backseat. Rivers and cheesy are two things that do not mix. "Fucking pussy whipped, cock sucking, pansy ass bitch," he mutters to himself, forcing Noah to spin around and nail him with everything he's got, giving Rivers a dead leg.

Tully leans forward over my chair, looping her arms around the headrest while ignoring the boys' scuffle beside her. "Get out. I'll take a photo of you with your sign."

Well, I'm not going to say no to that.

I push my way out of Noah's Camaro and suck in the fresh air, after being trapped in that car for hours on end with the boys competing in their morning farting ritual. Though, if I have to weigh in on the topic, I'd say it's too hard to pick a winner. Noah's got the whole loud but proud thing going on while Rivers takes on the silent but deadly. I guess the only losers here are me and Tully, especially after Noah hit the lock on the windows and made us suffer while they giggled like little school girls.

I make my way over to stand beneath the falling sign with an excitement pulsing through me. This is so freaking cool. I've never found a street sign with my name on it before.

Tully pulls out her phone as I hear the sound of Noah and Rivers' car doors opening, and to be honest, I'm freaking surprised that they didn't break a window or somehow destroy the car with their bullshit.

Rivers scoffs as the boys walk over. "If you really want to be her hero, then cut the fucking sign down and give it to her."

Noah looks across at Rivers before looking back at the sign with a sparkle in his eye. "Yeah?" he questions as a mischievous grin takes over.

"Yeah," Rivers replies.

"What? No," I shout out. "That's ridiculous and I'm pretty sure it's a felony. Besides, I'm not bailing your asses out of jail again."

"Again?" Tully grunts, straightening up and looking at me in confusion. "What the fuck do you mean 'again'?" Tully turns on Noah. "What the fuck is she talking about, Noah? You better not have been thrown in jail and not told me about it." she turns to Rivers. "Does that include you?"

"Fuck," I cringe, having completely forgotten that was supposed to be a secret. I look to the boys to see them scowling back at me. I give an innocent smile followed by a cringe. "My bad."

Rivers shakes his head as if to say 'don't worry about it' while Noah lets out a guilty sigh. "Yeah," he tells Tully. "Complete misunderstanding."

"Why do I feel like that's a lie?" she questions, studying

her brother with a practiced ease to be able to see right through him.

A sheepish look crosses his face. "Because it is."

"Just tell me it wasn't drugs."

"It wasn't drugs."

She looks to Rivers for confirmation and he gives her the slightest nod and it's almost as though, despite their current situation, she trusts his word even more so than her brother's, but I guess that's what happens when you love someone.

"So," Rivers says, moving the topic right along as he looks over at Noah. "You getting this sign or are you going to bitch out?"

Noah looks up and down the road, double checking that it's still deserted before shrugging a shoulder. "Yeah, alright. I'm in," he says, playing it cool. Though had I butted in and said that I desperately wanted it, Noah would have dove head first, straight into the challenge, not giving a shit if there was someone sharing the road with us or not.

He walks back to his car and rifles through the back, having to shuffle everyone's bags around first before pulling out a few tools. "You just keep that shit in the back of your car?"

He shrugs his shoulders as he strides back towards the street sigh. "Never know when you might need them," he tells me before he looks up and down the pole. "You just want the sign, right? Not the whole pole."

I look it over with a cringe, realizing I'm being difficult. "Well…the pole would be cool," I tell him. "I mean, it's not just going to magically float in the corner of my room, it needs a stand. Oh, maybe you could build little legs for it when we get home so it doesn't lean against the wall."

"Shit," he sighs as Rivers strides over to join him. The two of them fall into a murmured conversation. "How the fuck am I supposed to get the pole out? It's not like I have a fucking saw hidden in the back of my car, and now she wants fucking legs for it."

They put together a game plan as Tully rolls her eyes. "Are you dickheads forgetting that there's literally nowhere to put that thing in the car? What are you going to do? Strap it to the fucking roof?"

"Hey," Noah demands, turning back to Tully, pointing a finger at her. "Quit being such a downer or I'll leave you on the side of the fucking road. What my girl wants, my girl gets, and if she wants a fucking big ass pole with her name on it, then that's what's going to happen."

Rivers grins. "If the girl really wants a big ass pole, I've got one she could use."

Noah turns on Rivers with a lethal glare. "Fucking watch it, bro."

Twenty minutes later, the street sign balances on the center of the dashboard and goes right through to the back of the car, acting as some sort of line that separates Tully and Rivers, keeping them from clawing each other's eyes out.

The boys were lucky. The pole is that old that they were able to wiggle it around for a while and loosen the dirt around the base, after that, it just popped straight out as I watched on with a massive, cheesy grin. No one's ever broken a law for me before. It was kind of nice. Now I just got to make sure I don't get caught with it. No matter what though, this sign will always serve as a reminder of what an awesome time I've been having today, despite the rude wake up call.

Noah drives for another forty minutes before he turns down an old dirt road. "Is this it?" I ask, looking out the window but not able to see much as we're surrounded by bush.

"Think so," he says. "I haven't been here before, but from what I was told, we follow this road for about ten minutes and then turn down a little track and that should lead us into some kind of clearing. No one will bother us out here."

"It's kind of creepy," Tully murmurs, looking out the window just like the rest of us.

I don't look, but I can hear the smile in Rivers' tone. "You scared?"

"In your fucking dreams," she tells him with an irritated snap.

"It's ok, baby," he teases. "I'll keep you safe all night long."

"If you even look my way tonight, I'll castrate you. Got it?"

"Challenge accepted."

"Bullshit," she grumbles. "You're with Alyssa now and besides, you're too fucking pussy to come anywhere near me."

"And he better keep it that way," Noah rumbles from the front seat as I try to put myself in Rivers' position. One minute, Tully is telling him to keep away and the next, it's as if she's setting him a challenge to actually come after her. I guess it's a little hard for her to figure out what she actually wants from him right now.

I tune out their endless taunts and jabs and focus on the area around me. It's nothing short of beautiful. The trees are solid wood, not the shitty little, twig looking trees, but beautiful big ones that stand tall and proud. There are bushes, big and small, little creeks that flow through the land, a million different shades of rock, and I'm pretty sure I even see a walking trail.

Nothing is overgrown and it looks as though someone must spend a bit of time out here keeping the area clean, either that or there's some kind of killer hiding in the woods, spending his days pulling out weeds just waiting for idiots like us to show up. It's not like anyone would hear us scream out here. It would be the perfect area for mass murder. I hope Noah told someone where we were going. Is there phone signal out here? Maybe I should double check that.

Shit, that's probably not what I should be thinking about right before spending the night here in some flimsy tent. Though, I'm sure the boys would be more than willing to take down any threat that comes our way. Hell, if someone out here meant us harm, I'd even throw myself in, headfirst, ready to do some damage. There's nothing better than pummeling your fist into someone who deserves it. I haven't had a chance to do it in a while and my body is starting to crave it.

Hmmm. Maybe Noah would take one for the team. Nah, he's too pretty and I'd chicken out. I couldn't hurt him. Rivers though, he'd take it like a man and probably beg for more.

We pull up at the camping site and just as Noah had said, there's a big, open clearing, perfect for camping. There are trees all around to keep us hidden in case someone does come by, which is very unlikely. There's an area that's clearly been used for campfires, and tree stumps which have been placed around it, probably used as seating, though hopefully, Noah thought to bring some chairs as those stumps look fucking uncomfortable.

We get ourselves set up and to be honest, putting a tent together with Noah is something I never want to experience ever again. He's far too bossy and alpha for that shit. I left it to him and watched with a smirk as Rivers joined him and it quickly turned into an argument over who has the biggest set of balls.

Neither of them won. Tully had her tent up in half the time and sat back with a smirk, watching the show as she poured herself a well deserved drink. I guess reading the instructions has its benefits after all.

The day buzzes by in a relaxing, and incredibly amazing day. Who would have known that hanging out in the woods with nowhere to go would be so great? Tully and I escaped the boys and followed the little creek for a good twenty minutes and found that it came out into a huge pond or lake or whatever the hell it's called. All I know is that it had crystal clear water with perfect pebbles along the bottom. The sun glistened off it and it was simply radiant. We ended up going back and getting the boys before taking a swim and hoping to God that there were no weird creatures hiding within.

We gathered wood for the fire, we made ourselves a really shitty lunch, and we laughed. It was an incredible day. It gave me hope that maybe our little group could go back to normal. Tully and Rivers didn't fight from the second they stepped out of the car. You know, there were the normal little stabs here and there, but they came from a good place. It wasn't the ugly taunting and hating on each other that they've been doing lately.

The day has been incredible...until now.

The sun went down a little while ago and the chill has started to seep into the air. I pull my blanket more firmly around me, despite the fact that the fire has been burning strong for the past hour. I mean, it's doing a great job of keeping my legs warm, but the rest of me is starting to feel the cold. I'd brought my blanket and pillow over here purely for the whole comfort factor, but now I'm wondering if I should go and start rifling through my bag for a hoodie.

I pull my stick out of the fire before dunking my melted marshmallow in a cup of Bailey's and devouring it. Mmmm, now that's perfection. I thought Tully was going insane as I watched her dunk a marshmallow into the cup of Bailey's, but she insisted I try it and now there's no way I can go back to eating them plain. It's freaking delicious.

Rivers lays on the ground in front of the fire, propping his head up on his elbow, watching the flames before him as they light up his face. Noah sits beside me, hand held in mine as he plays with his phone in the other. A second later, he tosses the phone aside as music comes pouring out of the speakers, making the night that much better.

Noah looks up at his sister from across the fire. "You

never told us how your date with Rocko went?"

My eyes shoot down to Rivers who hasn't moved an inch. His eyes are still focused on the fire, but something tells me he's listening intently. Tully pushes another marshmallow onto the end of her stick before hovering it over the fire. "I didn't think you'd want to hear about it," she murmurs in a nervous tone, her voice barely audible over the soft crackling of the fire.

The fact that this is a dangerous topic isn't lost on anyone.

"Of course, I want to hear about it," Noah says. "You're my sister. I need to know if the guy is going to be hanging around and if I have to play nicely or if you realized what a fucking tool he is."

"He isn't a tool. He's actually kind of...sweet," she muses. "I mean, he's a bit rough around the edges and a bit cocky, but apart from that, he's ok."

And just like that, we all have our answer. Rocko won't be hanging around for long. She might try a few more times, see if she can build a connection with him, but looks like he'll just be mindless fun for now.

"Just ok?" Rivers murmurs.

"Just ok," she confirms, neither one of them looking at each other.

A breath escapes Noah and I glance over to see him struggling with whatever he's wanting to say. I squeeze his hand and his thumb instinctively rubs back and forth over my knuckles. He watches his sister silently for a moment. "Why are you dating him?"

"What do you mean?" she questions cautiously as Rivers sits up so he can read her expressions more clearly.

"Rocko. You don't like him. So, I don't understand why you're wasting your time with him when you're clearly in love with Rivers."

My mouth drops open as the four of us sit in silence, not one of us knowing what to do or say. It's like Voldemort.

It's the topic that is known but not talked about. Never talked about. Especially in this company.

Tully's breath comes in deeper as her eyes flick across to Rivers, both looking equally as shocked that Noah would say that or that he even knew how she felt. "It's true though, right? You love him?"

"I…" she looks back up at Noah. "I really don't want to talk about this."

"I think we should," he says. "Isn't that the whole point of us coming out here? To get everything out in the open so all this bullshit arguing can stop. I miss our fucking pack. So, what's it going to be, Tully? Do you love him?"

Her eyes flick back to Rivers and then to me before settling on Noah with a heavy brokenness that tears me apart. "Yes, ok. I do," she says as Rivers watches her closely. "I love him."

Noah nods. "How long?"

She lets out a small breath before a smile lifts the corner of her lips. "Years," she tells him.

"Why have you never told me?"

She shakes her head as though the answer is obvious. "Because he's your best friend, and besides," she adds, "I figured you always knew, just didn't want to hear about it."

"I guess I've always had my suspicions," Noah murmurs to himself. "So, why the whole Rocko bullshit? Why aren't you two together when he so clearly loves you too? It's not that hard to figure out."

Rivers shakes his head, not once denying Noah's claim. "It's not that easy, man."

"Why the hell not? Because of me?" he grunts. "What if I told you I'd give you both my blessing?"

My eyes widen just as Tully and Rivers do. "Fuck off, Noah," Rivers says, leaning back on his elbow as Tully watches the two men in her life like a tennis match. "Like hell you'd do that. Besides, it's more than that. I'd fucking be with her with or without your blessing and you know it.

It's more."

Noah raises his chin to Rivers. "Why the fuck didn't you tell me?"

"Because you don't want to hear that shit, not from me," he says, repeating the answer Tully had given him.

Noah shakes his head. We all know they're right on that one.

Noah watches the two as eyes continue flicking around the circle. "You're going to have to help me out here because I'm at a fucking loss," Noah says. "You're in love with each other but you're both fucking other people. It's clear as day that Alyssa and Rocko are just means to an end. Neither of you gives a shit about them and you clearly don't give a shit about me standing in the way, so, what's the fucking problem? 'Cause from where I'm standing, it looks like you're fucking hurting her for nothing."

"Noah," Tully says with tears in her eyes, gently shaking her head. "Please, just stop."

The boys completely ignore her and a pang rips through my heart for her. This can't be easy.

Rivers shoots to his feet and the movement has Noah moving right along with him. "You can't honestly stand there and tell me you wouldn't have a fucking problem with me dating your sister," he roars, getting in Noah's face as me and Tully slowly move in, hovering on either side of them, ready to step in if need be. "I'm fucking nothing and you know it. She needs better than this. She needs someone who can get her the fuck out of this shithole, give her the fucking world, not me."

I watch Noah's jaw clench. "You're really just going to screw her over like that? You two have been leading each other on for years and when it comes down to it, you're just going to bail like a fucking pussy."

"It's not that easy," Rivers repeats.

"So, what the hell happened then?" Noah demands. "You let her get close and then crush her just to put her in her place? Don't act like I don't fucking know all the times you two sneak off. You've been fucking her, haven't you? She's good enough to use, but not good enough to be with, is that it? She's not some fucking whore, she's my sister."

"Noah, stop," Tully demands, pulling at his arm.

"Answer the fucking question," Noah roars.

"Fuck," Rivers grunts. "It's not what you think."

"Are you fucking her? Yes or no."

"Noah," Tully demands, pulling at him once again. "Just…yes. Ok. Once. It happened once."

Crack.

Noah's arm shoots out like lightning, cracking hard across Rivers' jaw. Tully screams and dives for Rivers who flies backward, landing hard on his ass. I rush in front of Noah, grabbing his shoulders and forcing him to look at me. "You need to calm the fuck down before this gets out of hand."

"It's already out of hand," he seethes. "They're fucking sleeping together."

"Once," I tell him. "It only happened once."

Noah narrows is eyes on me and I realize my mistake. "You fucking knew about this?" he demands as betrayal pours from his features.

"I…yeah. I did, but it wasn't my place to say. This needed to come from them."

He shakes his head at me before brushing my hands off his shoulder. "Just fucking perfect," he mutters before walking away, leaving me standing behind feeling like absolute shit.

"Well," I say to Rivers and Tully who are in a messy heap on the floor as Tully tries to get a look at his jaw. "That went well."

CHAPTER 16

I stand by the fire with the blanket over my shoulders, pulling it tighter around me as I look out towards the dark woods for the hundredth time. Noah's been gone for over an hour and I'm starting to worry.

Nothing has really happened here apart from Tully drinking straight from the bottle of Vodka. Neither one of them have spoken a word. Each of them completely lost in their own mind, their feelings trampled and hearts hurting.

Rivers hand continues rubbing over his jaw but when he finally allowed us to get close enough, it was clear it wasn't broken. Though come tomorrow, there will be one hell of a nasty bruise.

"Noah just needs some time to cool down," I tell them. "He clearly suspected something had happened between the two of you, so he's probably more hurt that I kept it from him."

Tully gives me a grateful look, knowing I'm talking shit. We all know that while Noah is indeed pissed at me, that's not what's got him walking through the woods in the dark of

161

night.

I give her a tight smile. "You ok?" I question, making Rivers glance up for the first time in over an hour.

Tully shrugs a shoulder and presses her lips in a tight line before holding up the bottle of Vodka. "Will be when I finish this," she tells me.

Rivers lets out a breath and reaches across until his fingers curl around Tully's, silently letting her know she's going to be ok in a rare display of affection. I gape at their hands for a moment. Hearing them talk about it and seeing it up close and personal are two very different things. These two really are in love with each other. It's a damn shame they can't make it work.

Tully watches their hands too, but it's not with the same gaping that comes from me, it's a desperate longing for something more. He tugs on her hand and she instantly gets up, takes the step towards him, and drops down into his lap, burying her face into his neck as the tears start to fall.

Rivers' hand rubs up and down her back and I feel like I need to disappear inside my tent and give them a little privacy. I turn around and just as I start to head towards the tent, I see the light from Noah's flashlight app on his phone up in the distance.

I start walking towards him, hoping to God that it's actually him, otherwise this could go south very quickly. It's not long before we meet in the middle and his arms instantly wrap around me with his lips pressing against my forehead.

I close my eyes, soaking in the feel of his arms wrapped around me. "I'm sorry," I murmur into his chest, my words muffled by his shirt. "I wanted to tell you, but it wasn't my secret to tell. I've felt awful all this time."

"Shit," he says with a teasing tone. "All this time? How long ago did it happen?"

I pout up at him. "Don't ask me questions about it. Go and talk to them if you want details."

"I know, I will," he tells me before holding me a little

tighter. "I just need to make sure you're alright first."

"I'm fine," I tell him, raising my chin to press my lips to his. "But it's been one hell of an awkward hour since you stormed away."

"I bet," he smirks. "I probably shouldn't have punched him."

"Are you kidding?" I scoff. "He's your best friend and he slept with your sister then failed to tell you about it. He deserved it. Why do you think he didn't get up and fight? He took it. I bet he's been waiting for that punch since the moment he fell in love with her."

"You think?"

"Yeah," I sigh. "I do."

Noah looks up over my head before I feel his body go rigid. "It's like they're rubbing it in my face."

I look back over my shoulder to take in Tully still sitting on Rivers' lap with his arms wrapped securely around her. "No, they're not," I tell him. "She was hurting. She hates that you're upset with her and probably has a million awful things going through her mind. He's comforting her in the best way he knows how. Probably in the only way that could make her feel ok. It's what you'd do for me."

"They really do love each other, huh?"

"Yeah," I breathe, "more than I think they know."

"I should probably go talk to them."

"Yeah, I think Tully would like that," I tell him. "Just remember that despite you yelling at her and punching Rivers, she's still hurting from his rejection. It's fresh and that's why all this fighting is happening. She's an emotional mess so just…don't be too harsh on them, ok?"

"I won't," he says. "I think I got it all out of my system."

"Good," I smile, pulling out of his arms and taking his hand. "Then let's see if you can somehow get the answers out of Rivers that me and Tully have been failing to get."

"Is that a challenge?" he questions.

"As much as I want to say yes, I can't. I don't want you

to push the topic and make things worse for them."

He rolls his eyes. "As if I would do that."

"As if you wouldn't."

"Come on," he tells "Let's go get this over and done with so I can take you to bed."

"Now, that's a plan I can get on board with," I laugh as he starts pulling me back towards the campfire.

Neither Tully or Rivers look up from their embrace, but as if sensing us near, Rivers nudges Tully, and I guess out of respect for Noah, she moves back to her seat. Noah walks right up to Rivers and holds out a hand before they do one of those weird bro back clap things. "Sorry 'bout your face," he tells him with a grumble.

"It's fine," Rivers murmurs before dropping back down into his seat.

Noah walks around and takes the seat he was sitting in earlier as Tully watches him like a hawk. I sit down beside him, wrapping myself back up in my blanket and hating the weird tension that sits with us. "Alright," Noah sighs, looking up at Tully. "Start talking, and I want the long, drawn out version. Don't skip any details. I want to know exactly what's being going on behind my back."

She cringes as Rivers looks horrified, probably preparing himself for another fist in his jaw. After all, if Tully describes the dick piercing, I think we'll be packing up and heading straight to the hospital. "You don't mean…every detail, do you?"

"Fuck, Tully," Noah curses. "Everything except that."

I watch her whole body relax as Rivers lets out a shaky breath. "Oh, good. I was worried you were turning into some twisted, creepy perve then," Tully grins.

"Tullz," Noah snaps. "Get the fuck on with it. When did all this bullshit start?"

She turns to Rivers and gives him an apologetic smile, knowing that some of the things she says will probably make things worse, but it's now or never and this shit needs to be aired while it finally has a chance.

"It started the second you brought him home when we were eleven."

"The fuck?" Noah grumbles as Rivers turns to her with a proud, shit eating grin. "For real?" Rivers questions as cocky as ever. "I didn't know that."

"How could you?" she laughs. "You were a stupid boy with the biggest fucking ego. You walked through the door and winked, and that was it. I was a goner."

"Fuck, yeah, you were," River says, showing us exactly what Tully meant with the 'ego' comment.

"Can we get back on track?" Noah prompts.

Tully shrugs. "I guess…I don't really know what to tell you. Nothing really happened until a few weeks ago. Before that, it was nothing but the occasional flirting and chilling out, but you knew that." She looks across at Rivers with a smile in her eyes though her words are meant for Noah. "He's my constant. Always there. Protects me when you're not around, and not to mention, he's sexy as fuck. How could I not fall for him?" she continues. "I mean, we had a few weak moments that were generally brought on by alcohol, but nothing ever went further than making out."

Noah whips his head around to Rivers. "You didn't touch her until then?" he questions, clearly not giving a shit about the fact that they've been making out at parties, but I'm sure he would have known that already.

"Nope," Rivers says proudly. "Didn't touch her."

"Right," Noah murmurs slowly before turning back to Tully. "Go on."

"What can I say?" she shrugs, glancing across at me, knowing I already know what's coming next. "I'm not a patient girl. I got sick of waiting for him to come around, so I forced his hand. I told him exactly how I felt and didn't go stingy on the details."

Noah looks back at Rivers. "And you felt the same?"

Rivers eyes roam over Tully as she watches him before

reaching out and trailing his fingers over her arm. "How could I not? She's fucking beautiful."

Noah scoffs under his breath. "And you call me a fucking pussy whipped cunt," he murmurs, getting the side-eye from Rivers. "So, I'm assuming that's when," he scrunches his face up in disgust, "you know?"

"Yeah," Tully cringes.

"Fast forward past that shit. I want to know how the hell you two ended up fighting day in and day out, and I want to know why the fuck you've looked broken every time you've looked at him over the past few weeks."

Tully sighs, glancing up at her brother. "Do we have to?" she asks, looking across at me with pleading in her eyes, silently begging me to make her torture end. But I can't. Not this time. I'm on team Noah now. They've both kept this from him for so long and he deserves to know the truth.

"Just...please, Tullz. I know you don't want to talk about it, but I need to know. I promise I won't ask you about it again unless you want to talk."

She looks across at Rivers who looks as though the world is sitting on his shoulders. "You know, I'd change it if I could, right?" he tells her with his fingers still trailing over her arm.

"I know," she sighs before looking back at Noah. "The next morning, I woke up feeling like maybe we were going to make it work. I was over the fucking moon, but I got to school and the second I saw him, I just knew. He shut down and pushed me away, claiming that for some godforsaken reason that he wasn't good enough, and it fucking hurt like nothing before."

"That's what all those stupid dates and whoring around were about?"

"Yeah, but don't worry. It was all innocent, just a ploy to get under Rivers' skin, which I think was working by the way, until I decided that I wanted to hurt him right back and ended up fucking it all up."

Rivers scoffs as Noah narrows his eyes on her. "What do you mean?"

"Nothing," she says, glancing away.

"Nothing?" Rivers grunts in disbelief. "You fucking slept with Spencer. How is that nothing?"

"What?" Noah roars, flying to his feet. "Tell me that's a lie. Please, Tully, for all that is fucking holy, tell me it's a lie."

I cringe as let's be honest, there's really not a lot else I can do right now.

Tully sighs before looking across at me to avoid the gazes of the two angry as fuck men around her. "Alright," she says. "I've slept with him a few times. I dated him last summer and then slept with him again a few weeks ago at Kaylah's party."

That puts Rivers on his feet. "What?" he demands, his head spinning her way. "You never fucking told me you dated him last summer."

Tully's not finished yelling though. "What's the big fucking deal?" she throws back at Rivers, giving him just as much attitude as he threw her way. "It's not like you tell me about all the whores you've been with, and believe me, from the stories I hear coming left, right, and center, there's a fucking lot of them."

I smother a chuckle and resist fist bumping her. That shut him down.

"Wait," Noah throws in. "Don't tell me you're not with her now because of Spencer?"

Rivers growls. "It's got nothing to do with him. I was pissed about it for all of thirty seconds."

Tully looks back at Noah. "Can we please get back on track?"

I grab the back of his shirt and pull him back until he's sitting down once again. "Fine," he grunts, "but for the record, I'm not fucking happy about this."

Tully salutes him just to get on his nerves. "Noted," she smirks before continuing. "So, just when I thought he was finally coming around, Rivers overheard me telling Henley about Spencer-"

"Whoa," Noah butts in, his head swiveling towards me. "You knew about this too?"

Damn it. "Of course, I fucking knew," I snap back at him. "She's my girl."

"Noah," Tully yells. "Get the fuck over Spencer. This is about me and Rivers."

"Fine. Whatever."

She lets out a frustrated huff but goes on. "So, he heard what happened with Spence and that was it, it was over before it even began, but I guess I was stupid to think that there was still a small chance. After all, it didn't take a genius to work out that he'd regretted being with me."

"Whoa," Rivers cuts in, demanding her complete, full attention. "Hold the fuck up, babe. I don't regret it. Not one fucking bit," he tells her.

"But-"

"No," he growls. "How could you possibly think that?"

"You don't want to be with me," she throws back at him. "No matter what your excuses are, you pushed me away. What the hell did you think was going to go through my head? All this time you keep telling me that you're not good enough, but all that does is make me feel not good enough."

"Fuck, no, babe." Rivers grabs her chair and spins her around to face him straight on. "I told you this was about me," he demands. "Not fucking you. Never you. You're fucking perfect. I didn't fall in love with you and put us through all this bullshit for you to come out the other end feeling like that."

Tears fill her eyes. "So, you just decided for us then? That we don't even get a shot? It'll never happen?"

Rivers shakes his head. "I don't see how."

Damn it. I can't watch this.

I turn to Noah, pulling on his hand. "Come on," I tell him. "Have you heard what you need to hear yet? We should go. Give them a chance to talk this all through."

"Yeah," he says, glancing back at them one more time. "That sounds like a fucking great idea."

With that, we get up and I fumble around with my blanket and pillow before Noah rolls his eyes and scoops me up off the ground so I don't have to bother unwrapping myself.

He makes his way into the tent and suddenly, the night that I've been dreaming about all day seems so far away. It's not even my relationship that's being discussed, but for some reason, I feel emotionally drained.

I let out a heavy sigh as Noah drops me down into our makeshift bed. "You ok?" he murmurs, coming down beside me and drawing me into his arms.

"Yeah," I grumble, "that was just a bit...heavy."

"I know," he murmurs as I nuzzle my face into his chest. "Are you ok? That couldn't have been easy." I feel him shrug and find myself lifting my head back up at looking at him. "You want them to be together, don't you?" I question. "That's why you were pushing it so hard."

"I don't know, maybe," he admits. "It's just...you saw how he was looking at her out there. He adores her. I don't know how I haven't seen that before. No other motherfucker out there is going to look at her and treat her the way that he would."

"They're perfect together," I agree. "I just wish he'd pull his head out of his ass and do something about it."

"I don't know," he muses. "Rivers isn't the kind of guy to easily change his mind. Once he's set on something, that's it. If he doesn't feel worthy of her, then she might as well start looking elsewhere."

"I don't like the sound of that," I tell him. "I want them to be happy, like us."

"I know," he murmurs. "As much as it kills me to say it, I do too."

The sun comes streaming through the flimsy fabric of the tent and I peel my eyes open. It's freaking cold but with Noah's arms wrapped around me, it doesn't seem so bad. Hopefully, the sun will do its thing soon and warm me enough to function.

We're well and truly into winter now, so I guess it was our stupid fault for going camping, but with the promise of sleeping in Noah's arms and a campfire, it really didn't seem so bad. I didn't take into account what it would be like waking up in a tent with no hot coffee or heating.

It's not like it snows here, so I really shouldn't be complaining. Others have it much worse, but still, my nipples are hard and it's not because of the hand that's currently cupping my tits.

I lay, nestled in Noah's arms until the urge to pee completely takes over. I start getting up and Noah instantly pulls me back down to him. "Where are you going?" he says in his all too sexy morning voice, though, that isn't the only morning thing he's got going on right now.

I push out of his arms once again but this time he puts up a better fight. "I have to pee," I tell him, the overwhelming need getting a little more serious than I can handle.

"Fine," he groans, not bothering to open his eyes. "But you better come straight back. I haven't heard you scream my name yet."

Damn, that sounds good.

I make my way out of the tent and hurry into the woods before the threat of pissing myself becomes all too real. I give myself a metaphorical pat on the back when I manage to pee once again without destroying my clothes before waltzing back into the clearing and heading for our tent.

Movement across the clearing has me glancing up to find Tully dawdling back from the opposite side of the woods, probably after taking her own morning wee. She walks forward, still not having seen me and my eyes flick between her and the tent which holds the promise of one hell of a good morning.

Tully. Noah. Tully. Noah.

Shit.

I turn towards Tully and start heading her way. Her head finally comes up a few steps away and she gives me a bright smile. "Good morning," she smiles, dropping down in front of the cooler and rifling through until she pulls out a bottle of water. "Want one?" she questions.

"Nah, I'm good," I tell her as I take my seat from last night and poke a stick around the burnt out ashes from the campfire. The fire is well and truly gone but I can't help but notice the lingering smell as I push it all around. "How'd you go last night?" I ask as she drops down in the chair beside me.

"Before or after we fought? Or before or after he kissed me?"

I grin across at her, knowing just how much she would have liked that. "All of it."

Tully presses her lips together, deep in thought as she goes over her night with Rivers, making me wonder if maybe it isn't as good as what I think it is. "I think it's all good," she finally tells me. "We talked, and while nothing has changed, I don't feel as though I need to tear him apart every time I see him."

"I guess that's a start," I murmur, wondering how the hell they could go from that to him kissing her.

"Yeah, I think I've been doubting how he actually feels about me like as though saying he wasn't good enough was just some kind of excuse, but he's hurting just as much as I am. He feels it like I do."

"That's what I've been trying to tell you," I smile, feeling a little cocky but doing a great job not letting it show. "He loves you, but what does that mean moving forward?"

She shakes her head and I see the hurt still lingering in her eyes. "It means nothing," she says. "He's not prepared to jump headfirst into this with me, so I guess I'm left with the 'trying to move on plan'."

"Rocko?" I question.

"Yep, and he'll be staying with Alyssa, silently killing me every time I see them together."

"Maybe it's not a great idea to be dating Rocko. I don't think your heart is ready yet."

"I need something to distract me from the thought of his tongue down her throat instead of mine."

"Shit," I sigh. "Maybe you should both just stop dating."

"I can't ask him to do that," she says. "Just because he's not mine, doesn't mean he can't try to find happiness somewhere else. That's not fair."

A body barges between us before Rivers bends down and presses a kiss to the side of her face. "Yes, you can," he murmurs. "Just say the word and I'll stop. I won't do it if it's hurting you."

Tully presses her hand into his and he pulls her out of the chair before walking away, side by side, clearly with still a little more to discuss.

"You never came back," a deep, accusing voice murmurs from behind me.

I turn in my seat to find a pair of green eyes staring into mine with nothing but a mischievous smirk on his face, and considering the large bulge currently tenting the front of his sweat pants, I have a damn good feeling what he's got planned for me. I shrug my shoulders and give him an innocent smile. "Yeah, well, you never took me on a date."

I wait for the usual 'I knew that was going to come back and bite me on the ass' comment that always seems to get thrown around, but when something else comes shooting from his mouth, I find myself gasping and clenching my thighs in anticipation.

"Henley Fucking Bronx," he warns so low that the sound shoots straight down to my lady bits. "Get that fine ass of yours back to that tent, and when I get there, you better be wearing not a goddamn thing, on your hands and knees with your ass up in the air, ready and waiting for me."

Fuck me. I think I stare at him a moment too long before scrambling to my feet and hurrying to the tent. I've done a few stupid things in my life, but not offering myself up on a platter to Noah Cage when he's ready to put it down is not going to be one of them.

A moment later, I'm ready and waiting just as he told me too. And when he comes in and curls his hand around my hair, holding me still, I bite down on my lip knowing I better hold on tight for one hell of a wild ride.

CHAPTER 17

Aria sits between me and Tully at their breakfast table while Violet busily runs around the kitchen, putting things away before we all have to get out of here in about ten minutes.

I try to force a little more breakfast down Aria's throat, you know, all that 'breakfast is the most important meal of the day' stuff that parents, teachers, and doctors are always going on about. I mean, there has to be some sort of merit in that, but just to be sure, I grab a few more slices of fruit and add them to the pile on her plate.

"Would you quit trying to feed the kid?" Tully grumbles around a piece of toast. "She'll be the size of an elephant if you don't let up."

"She's fine," I grumble. "She's like me. She loves her food."

"Exactly, and just like you, she'll end up with a tummy ache."

Damn it. She's probably right.

Oh well. I add another slice of toast to her plate just in

case. Besides, what happens if she forgets to eat her lunch at school? I wouldn't want her getting hungry, though something tells me lunch is Aria's favorite part of the day.

Noah comes striding in with a grin on his face and a twinkle in his eye before silently bending down and pressing a kiss to my cheek. He takes a seat beside Rivers, minding his own business as he goes about pouring himself a coffee and refilling mine and Tully's.

"Yo," Rivers says pushing up out of his chair, letting it scrape loudly against the tiles before taking his plate over to the sink and rinsing it off. "I'm out."

"Huh?" Tully grunts, checking the time. "You never leave this early."

"Yeah, umm…"

"You're picking up Alyssa," she says, finishing his sentence while looking down at her plate, though something tells me she just lost her appetite.

Rivers hovers in the kitchen for a long pause. "I don't have to," he murmurs, suddenly more at ease when talking about their feelings though I guess that happens when all their dirty laundry is forced out in the open.

"You're not dating me, Rivers. You're dating her. Go and pick the girl up."

His eyes linger on her for a moment before he lets out a silent breath and walks away. No one says a word as we hear him walk through the house, collect his car keys, and then stride through the front door. All while Noah's grin gets wider.

"You ok?" I murmur, looking to Tully to double check she's not about to break.

The front door is barged in and Noah flies to his feet with only moments to spare before Rivers' body slams him into the wall. The two of them go down to the ground, fists flying as they try to get the best of the other, Noah unable to control his howling laughter.

"What are you doing?" Violet shrieks as Noah's dad,

175

Eddison, hurries in to try and break them up.

Tully gapes at them while I watch on in suspicion. Noah was far too happy walking in here before. He was up to something and the sparkle in his eyes was the dead giveaway.

"Cut it out," Eddison says, finally pulling them apart, though I don't know how he's capable of such a thing. He must be some kind of superhero with strength as his power because as far as I'm concerned, getting between these two during a fight is impossible and will most likely result in a death wish. "What the hell is going on?" Eddison scolds. "You're scaring Aria."

All eyes fall to Ari to find her standing on her chair, wide-eyed with a huge grin on her face. "Goooooo Rivers!" she squeals. Yeah, that's my girl. You've got to be tough if you live in Haven Falls otherwise you simply won't make it. I learned that the hard way. Aria though, she was just born tough. I have a feeling she's seen more than the rest of us combined.

"Yeah, really scared," Noah grins as Rivers continues to scowl.

"Will somebody please tell me what the hell is going on?" Tully cuts in. "I thought you had better things to do."

Rivers' eyes swivel to Noah. "I would be doing better things except there's a massive, bright pink, ten inch, rubber dildo duct taped to my fucking hood."

"What?" Tully barks out, gaping again before the uncontrollable laughter claims her.

"I got to see this," I laugh, briefly wondering where the hell Noah had a bright pink dildo stashed and if I need to be concerned about him. I mean, there are some things I'm willing to do behind closed doors, but there's definitely a limit to how crazy I'll get. A ten inch dildo...maybe not. I'd prefer the real thing.

I make a break for the door with Tully barging out right behind me as I hear Aria in the kitchen singing, "Dildo, dildo, dildo."

Fuck. That's going to be a hard one to explain to my father.

The second I step out the door, the cold morning wind hits me, but I power on. There's no way I'm about to miss this. My eyes quickly search out Rivers' Firebird that sits right at the top of the drive and swaying proudly from left to right in the wind, is indeed, a massive, pink rubber dildo, and let me tell you, it's definitely more than ten inches.

I stand and gape at Rivers' new hood ornament, Tully rolls around on the ground, clutching her stomach while howling with laughter, Noah smirks from beside me as though he's the proudest motherfucker around, while Violet desperately tries to hold Aria back, refusing to let her see what the hell a dildo is.

This day could not get any better. I swear, some kind of natural disaster could rip through here and the memory of this pink dildo will still manage to keep a smile on my face.

Noah's hand slips into mine and I look up at him as he watches Rivers manhandle the thing, trying to pull it off...and not in the good way. "Do I even want to know where you've been hiding that thing?"

Noah looks down at me before sending a devastatingly sexy wink my way. "Would you think differently of me if I told you it was in my bedside table?"

"I guess it depends on why it was there?" I laugh, raising a suspicious, accusing eyebrow.

"Hey," he warns. "I like chicks."

"Uh huh."

Tully calls out to Rivers, dragging my attention from my possibly closeted boyfriend. "You're being too rough," she tells him. "He doesn't like it."

"Fucking watch it," Rivers snaps back at her.

"Do you need some help?" she grins wickedly. "I can show you a few things."

"Fuck me," Noah groans beside me

Rivers eventually gets the dildo unstuck and does so

without recruiting Tully's help, though my guess is that it was a pride thing or maybe he just wanted to prove to the world that he could handle the big fucker. Who knows?

Our morning pretty much gets back to normal and before I know it, I'm sitting in Mr. Carver's biology class, looking down at the completed scholarship application form on my desk in front of me.

The end of class bell sounds but I hang back in my chair, waiting for the students to file out as Tully waits by the door. "Ah, you filled it all out?" Mr. Carver inquires fondly.

"Yep, I sure did," I tell him.

"Great timing," he says before digging through the papers on his desk. "I printed off your recommendation just an hour ago and spoke with your other teachers. They're all working on their plans to get you the extra credit you need, and hopefully, we can make this happen."

"Thank you," I say as he hands me the recommendation. My eyes desperately want to look down and read through it, but with the guy standing right before me, it feels a little too personal. I'll read it when I get home.

"No drama," he tells me, walking back to his desk and organizing his things. "There should be some instructions on the application detailing how they expect it to be submitted, so make sure you do all that and let me know how it goes."

Wow. Ok, shit. This is actually happening.

"Thanks," I tell him again. "I'll go over it at lunch and get it submitted."

"Good work, Henley," he tells me. "You deserve it."

With that, I file out of the room until Tully is looping her arms through mine. "Well, let's see it then," she tells me, slipping the recommendation out of my fingers. "It's almost unbelievable that someone here would have something good to say about you."

"Shut up," I laugh. "I'd like to see any of the teachers here give you a recommendation."

"Whatever," she huffs. "I don't need a recommendation

178

from those bitches to know how fucking cool I am. All I have to do is walk into a room."

I roll my eyes as she scans over the recommendation. "Ugh, are you sure Carver just isn't trying to get into your pants?" she says, taking in what he's written.

"Get lost," I tell her, snatching the letter back out of her fingers. "He is not. He's just trying to help his students make something of themselves."

"Yeah, after he gets a slice of your cherry pie."

"Geez," I groan. "It's no wonder your brother hasn't adopted you out yet."

"I know. We've gotten close a few times, but he just can't seem to get rid of me."

"Oh well, here's to hoping."

The rest of the day goes by in some kind of a blur and before I know it, I'm walking down to the student parking lot, searching out Noah's car, but not able to find it anywhere. "Where's Noah?" I ask Rivers as he drops down in his car beside the spot Noah usually parks in.

"On a job," he tells me.

"What?" I grunt, my head whipping towards him. "Without you?"

"Yeah, no big deal," he says though the look in his eyes suggests otherwise. "We go solo all the time."

I scrunch up my face. "I don't know if I like that."

"You don't gotta like it," he tells me. "Just deal with it knowing he'll come see you as soon as he's done. Now, get your ass in. I'm taking you girls home."

Well, that's one way to shut down the conversation.

Tully walks down and comes straight over to Rivers' car as though she already knew he was taking us home. I let her take the front and when Rivers doesn't instantly start reversing out of his spot, Tully snaps at him. "What are you doing, dickwad? Get a move on."

Rivers face scrunches up in a way that I've never seen before. "Don't hate me, ok," he begs, turning to Tully. "I sort of promised Alyssa I'd drop her home too."

Tully's face falls. "Get fucked," she growls before reaching for the door handle.

"No, don't," Rivers says, latching onto her arm and pulling her back. "Don't go. She only lives around the corner. She'll be out of here before you know it. I don't want you walking home. It's too cold."

"So, I've got to sit in here and watch you walk her to the door. Kiss her goodbye. Yeah fucking right."

"Come on, Tullz," he says. "You're the one who said you're cool with this. You're still dating Rocko." He lets out a breath. "I promise. I won't walk her in."

"Whatever," she says, staring out the window and pointedly looking away, especially when Alyssa strides down and climbs into the car.

She looks cautiously to me and Tully before leaning over into the front seat and pressing a kiss to Rivers' cheek. "Thanks," she says. "You didn't have to take me home."

Tully looks back with her perfect bitch face. "Then walk."

"Ignore her," Rivers murmurs, instantly backing the car out of the spot so no one has a chance to get out. I know, I'm probably the safest bet as to which of us girls is more willing to be here right now, but the level of tension radiating around this car has me wanting to be the one to Superman dive out the door. I've never done it before and I'm sure as hell it would hurt, but I'm willing to take the risk.

It's like ice cold in here and I don't mean because of the weather.

I pull out my phone.

Henley – You're in so much trouble for leaving me to deal with this stupid Tully/Rivers/Alyssa love triangle bullshit.

Noah – Why? What happened now?

Henley – Rivers promised to drive Alyssa home as well.

Noah – Fuck. Hide anything sharp. Either Rivers or

Alyssa are about to meet their maker. I'll make it up to you when I get home.

Henley – K. Love you.

Noah – Fucking love you too, Spitfire.

Just as Rivers had said, Alyssa lives nearby and we're at her place in the blink of an eye. She leans forward into the front to say goodbye, but this time goes for Rivers' lips.

Tully's eyes narrow on the girl and her hand reaches for a fistful of hair.

I move faster than lightning. My hand shoots out and the loud sting of my hand slapping against Tully's is heard throughout the car, but lucky for us, neither Rivers or Alyssa can figure out where it came from.

I give Tully a nasty look and she shoots one right back, more than pissed that I stole her opportunity to take a bitch down.

As Rivers promised, he doesn't walk her to the door, but he waits patiently for her to walk inside her home before he pulls away from the curb and looks over to Tully. "Thank you," he murmurs quietly.

"For what?"

"Being on your best behavior."

We both scoff. If nearly ripping out chunks of hair is his definition of best behavior, then yeah, she did great.

The tension disappears from the car and we get on our way. Tully turns up the music, I sit back and sing along, while Rivers steals sneaky glances at the scary as shit, badass woman sitting beside him.

He brings the car to a stop at a red light and waits patiently as Tully blabbers on about her day, though I don't doubt he's hanging on every word she says. He hits the gas and moves forward across the intersection as the light turns green.

"FUCK!," he yells, swerving across the road and throwing his arm up in front of Tully's chest.

My eyes snap up to the road to take in the red car,

speeding through the red light and careening towards. "NO," I scream as my heart instantly begins to race.

The last thing I hear is Tully terrified gasp before the car smashes into us, sending us hurtling across the intersection and slamming into a tree.

My head spins.

In and out of consciousness.

It's hard to breathe.

My chest.

Noise sounds all around me as a strange smell stings my nose. I try to peel open my eyes and blink back a few times. The world continues spinning around me but the sound of Rivers' voice cutting through the fog has me finally able to zone in on him.

I lay on the rocky asphalt, my body burning from…something. "No, baby. Don't you dare go to sleep. Keep your eyes on me," Rivers begs with tears in his eyes.

I focus more.

Tully is cradled in his arms as blood pours from a gash on his forehead.

She was closest to the tree.

Panic tears through me and my eyes flutter closed before I force them open once again.

Sirens sound in the distance and I keep my eyes trained on Tully, waiting for her to move, but the last thing I see before completely passing out is her body falling limp in Rivers' arms.

CHAPTER 18

The constant beep of the monitor makes the raging storm inside my head unbearable and has me peeling my eyes open despite my better judgment.

The room is too bright. Big clinical lights shine down on me from above as that awful hospital smell hits me. Shit. What have I done to land myself here?

That's right. The car crash.

Tully.

Fuck.

Movement has my eyes flicking across the room to take in the three large bodies sitting at the end of my bed. "Henley," Noah sputters out, flying to his feet and rushing forward as he notices my eyes are open. His movement has Dad's head whipping in my direction before relief settles over his features. While Rivers remains still, looking completely deflated.

"How are you feeling?" Noah rushes out as Dad gets to his feet and comes to my other side. Both of them grabbing a hand each.

"How long was I out?" I murmur, hating how the sound of my own voice makes my head feel that much worse. "How bad is it?"

Noah cringes, not wanting to answer, but dad has no reservations. "You hit your head pretty bad, Squish. You're pretty cut up, but nothing you can't handle," he says before glancing up at the clock. "The ambulance brought you in about two hours ago."

"Damn," I grumble.

"How are you feeling?' Noah repeats.

"I could use some painkillers," I tell him, making his hand squeeze mine. "My head is pounding."

Dad cuts in. "I'll get the nurse. Hopefully she'll just dose you up and I can get you home in your own bed."

Damn, that sounds so good.

A moment later, Dad's rushing out the door and I follow his movements as he passes Rivers. I can't help but linger there, watching as his head hangs low. A vision of Tully laying limp in Rivers' arms flashes through my head and is enough to have me trying to get out of bed to go searching for her. "Tully?" I question as Noah tries to push me back down in my bed. "Tell me she's alright," I say with tears brimming in my eyes. "Where is she?"

Rivers' head raises just a bit. "She's in surgery," he says, his voice coming out as barely a whisper.

The red light. The tree. She was sitting right where we hit the tree. Oh, God. No. If I'm this banged up, then she must be...

No.

A sob gets stuck in my throat as I clench down on Noah's hand, looking up into the eyes that are so much like his sister's. "Is she ok?" I beg, fearing the worst.

He shakes his head and I see the need within him to break. Hospital rooms and sisters are all too familiar for him. The last time he was in one, he lost his little sister. It can't happen again. I don't know what kind of man he would be if he walked out of this hospital an only child. It would change him forever.

He's trying to be strong for me, but doesn't he know he doesn't need to?

"Noah," I prompt, needing to know how bad it is.

When Noah struggles to get it out, Rivers sighs a sound that I'll never forget as long as I live. "She has extensive internal blee-"

"NO," Noah roars at him through the too small room, his voice sounding like a hammer against my skull. He strides across the room, grabbing Rivers in a heartbeat and slamming him up against the wall. "You don't get to respond. You don't get to have a damn fucking thing to do with her after this. She's on that fucking table because of you. You put her there."

"Fuck you," Rivers growls, pushing him back. "If you didn't try to be a fucking hero and take that job, you would have been there, driving her home yourself."

Noah slams his fist into Rivers' gut. "Oh, so this is my fucking fault?"

Rivers pushes him back and the two of them crash into the end of my bed. "You could have fucking killed her," Noah roars. "Both of them."

Shit. This is more than just a fight. This is as real as it gets. If they're not careful, they're going to get hurt and it's not going to be pretty.

"Don't you think I know that?" Rivers yells back at him. "You weren't fucking there. I was the one who pulled her out of that fucking car while she was drowning in her own blood. Do you have any idea what that was like? No. So, don't stand there telling me what could have fucking happened, because I know too fucking well."

"Stop," I yell, throwing the blankets back and storming out of bed, only to get caught on the fucking drip pulling at my wrist. "Both of you fucking idiots. Stop it."

Naturally, they couldn't give a shit what I have to say

about it.

The door of my room is barged in with my Dad storming towards the boys with about three doctors, a few nurses, and some guy who probably shouldn't be here.

They instantly start scuffling around, trying to break it up. Dad clocks a shoulder to the face, a doctor gets shoved into a wall, and some old bat gets pushed and tumbles onto my bed before they can manage to get it under control.

"Right, you," Dad says, grabbing Rivers by the scruff of his shirt. I almost want to laugh at the sheer ridiculousness of it. Dad is a big guy, but Rivers still towers over him. "Get the fuck out of here. You can go and wait for Tully with the rest of her family." Dad practically barges him out of the room and I'm surprised as hell when he doesn't put up a fight.

"As for you," Dad says to Noah. "Keep your shit under control. I know you're stressed about your sister, but this room right here is about the health of my daughter. If you can't, you can go and fuck off too."

Noah nods his head and takes a deep breath before dropping down on the chair he had been in earlier, probably with a million thoughts flying through his head, some old, but definitely some new ones too.

"Now, Squish," Dad says turning to me. "Why the fuck are you out of bed? Get your ass in there so the doctor can look you over."

I quickly nod and scramble back into bed. Dad hasn't had to pull out his 'Dad' voice in years and honestly, it's kind of terrifying.

He drops down into the chair beside Noah as he mumbles to himself. "It's like dealing with a bunch of fucking children."

With that, the doctor turns to me as a nurse tends to the drip in my wrist which apparently is half out and looking a little like a murder scene with the way I've been flailing about. Who would have known?

Observations. Concussion. Unknown dangers. Ok, I fucking get it. I have to stay here longer than I thought, but so far, we're creeping up to the thirty hour mark and it's killing me. Don't get me wrong, I know the medical professionals know what they're talking about and all that shit, but I just want to be home in bed, watching Netflix while Frog goes 'round and 'round in her bowl.

Is that too much to ask?

Tully was in surgery for about four hours and was left in recovery for a few more after that. Noah didn't want her all the way over there and put up a fuss, insisting she would heal better if she had her friends with her, so here we are, our beds side by side in a squishy room.

We just have to be thankful that we're not in some ward with a hundred other people. Though, it could also have something to do with the fact that it's an overcrowded hospital with not enough rooms. I have no idea how we swung a private room though, but if I had to guess, I'd say the boys had something to do with that too.

We haven't seen Rivers since dad kicked him out, meaning Tully hasn't seen him at all since she woke up and I know that's hurting her. Her family has come and is always nearby, people from school keep knocking on the door as though they have some right to be here, the side of the room is filled with balloons and flowers, and we're both fucking sick of it.

I mean, if visitors want to bring something, then they should be bringing McDonalds or something to really get our blood pumping, not these stupid reminders of the hell we went through. Tully is sore and broken, she doesn't need all these people in here watching her heal. Hell, I'm lucky that I get to be so close. I think Noah worked that out pretty early on as after the tenth time a person came knocking, he told them to fuck off and leave her alone. The nurses quickly got the gist and stopped giving out the room number.

Having Tully in the same room means that I get an up close, detailed explanation of her injuries. Not that she wouldn't have told me anyway, but it's nice hearing it firsthand from the doctors and be able to hear their take on her recovery. During the crash, her right arm was crushed and her head was hit, causing a slight fracture to her skull. Three ribs broke and a piece of rib punctured a lung while she also suffered internal bleeding.

The doctors are saying she's lucky to be alive and I have to say, I agree with them. I only suffered a nasty headache which is nearly gone now and am a little cut up. I don't know why they're keeping me here this long, but it could possibly have something to do with the fact that it's good for Tully, to help her heal. Not that it's going to happen overnight, but I've been keeping her spirits up and making sure there's a smile on her face.

I know, I know, I'd want me around too.

Noah's phone lights up with a text and not a moment later, he walks out the door, leaving Tully and I alone for the first time in ages. I look over to her as she scoffs. Her voice comes out croaky and rough but she's too proud to pull back. "After the hell I've been through, he better not be leaving to go do a job."

I can't help but look to the door, following where he's just excited. "Nah, he wouldn't," I say, a little unsure, eyes narrowing. "Surely, he wouldn't."

"This is Noah we're talking about," she grumbles.

I hear her bed sheets ruffling and whip my head back around to her. "What do you think you're doing?" I shriek as she tries to reach for the cup of water sitting by her bed. "You're going to tear your stitches."

"I'm fine," she grumbles.

I shake my head and roll out of bed, before stepping across to her, hoping I don't rip out my drip again. I mean, that shit wasn't fun. I grab Tully's water and hold the little straw up to her. "You could have just asked," I tell her.

She takes the sip of water and I see it in her eyes, she hates this. She doesn't like feeling weak and broken, but she sure as hell wasn't going to show it in front of her tough as nails brother. "How're you feeling?" I question, knowing now's probably the only time I'll get a straight answer out of her.

"I feel like a truck ran over me and then backed up just to make sure the job was done."

"That bad?" I murmur, holding up the water again so she can take another sip. "You know, it's perfectly acceptable to ask for stronger pain meds."

She scrunches up her face and I step over to hit the button on my bed which calls in the nurse. "What are you doing?" she grumbles, hardly able to put up much of a fight.

"I'm getting you sorted out seeing as though you won't do it yourself," I tell her, straightening up her sheets to make her a little more comfortable, the same way her mom had been doing before she left. "Besides, the strong stuff is good. It's like taking a mini vacation."

She rolls her eyes as the nurse comes strolling in. Her eyes flick to me, assuming I'm the one who needs her before looking across at Tully. The nurse doesn't curse me out on the fact that I'm not in bed and I thank her for it. Besides, I'd have a thing or two to say about it if she wanted to try.

"What do you need dear?" she asks as she checks over Tully's chart.

I speak up for her. "She needs stronger pain meds but she's too tough to admit it and ask for it."

The nurse gives Tully a stern look before raising a questioning brow. "You're only making it harder for yourself if you fight the process the whole way along."

"Fine," Tully murmurs. "I feel like shit. My legs are cramping. I want to take a shower. My head hurts, and my body aches, and if someone doesn't take this catheter out of me soon, I'm going to scream."

The nurse takes a slow breath. "I see," she says. "Well, unfortunately, there's nothing I can do about the catheter, that needs to stay until you can get yourself up and walking around. The shower...again, up and walking around. Everything else, I can handle."

With that, she excuses herself and returns a few minutes later with a little tray filled to the brim with the good stuff. "Oooh, can I have some of that?" I smirk, sitting on the edge of my bed and looking at the party mix before me. It's like a guessing game; what will happen if I take the blue one?

The nurse shakes her head and 'tsk's' me. "I don't even know why you're still here," she says. "You're clearly fine."

I shrug my shoulders. "I guess they're keeping me around for the entertainment."

"That seems about right," she chuckles before getting Tully sorted.

She makes her way out of the room just as Noah barges back in. I look down at Tully and wink, letting her know she just got away with murder. She got her pain meds and admitted feeling like shit all without anyone knowing.

Noah strides in and standing in the middle of the room looking awkward for a brief moment. I'm about to ask what crawled up his ass when a figure walks through the door behind him.

Rivers.

His eyes fly straight to Tully and he looks completely shattered.

Complete silence.

There's no other way to describe it...apart from awkward as fuck.

Noah's eyes finally come to mine and if finally realizing what's right in front of him, he completely loses his shit. "Why the fuck are you out of bed?" he roars, pulling my attention away from the devastation on Rivers' face.

"Oh, shut up," I scold with a roll of my eyes. "I was helping your sister get a drink of water to avoid her getting out of bed."

Noah's eyes flick right back to Tully's. "Excuse me?" he sputters but she doesn't respond. It's as though she's locked in some kind of trance with Rivers. The two of them haven't even blinked since he walked in.

There are a million things that need to be said here, but I have to admit, what comes out of her mouth, is the one thing I wasn't expecting. "How's your girlfriend?"

Rivers' eyes widen like saucers. "Fuck," he grunts in horror. "I forgot about her."

A grin rips across Tully's face. "You know, that almost makes all of this worth it."

He shakes his head as Noah and I watch on in confusion. How could they possibly be discussing this right now? Rivers pulls his phone out of his pocket and goes to text her when thinking better of it. "Fuck it," he says, tossing the phone onto the end of my bed. "I'll talk to her later."

With that, he walks over to the side of Tully's bed and takes her hand in his before leaning forward and pressing the softest kiss I've ever seen to her lips. "You've got to know how sorry I am," he murmurs.

"It wasn't your fault," she tells him, tears brimming in her eyes as she raises a hand to his cheek. "You couldn't have known that car was going to run a red light. This isn't on you."

Noah walks over to me and takes my hand before grabbing the stand for my drip. "Come on," he tells me, slipping an arm around me despite the fact that I don't need it. "Let's give them a moment."

I couldn't agree more.

Noah takes me out and pulls me down on his lap in a chair just outside my room. He nuzzles his face into my neck. "Fuck, I want to take you home."

"Seriously?" I laugh, trying to be quiet as to not disturb the other patients. "I was just in a car crash and your thinking about getting nasty?"

I feel his grin against my skin. "I meant get you out of the hospital, you dork. I don't like seeing you here." Oh. "Who's the one with the dirty mind now?"

"Whatever," I grumble, rolling my eyes. "I'm hoping they'll discharge me soon, but I want to stay with Tully."

"I know," he murmurs. "I think she likes having you with her and it probably helps that you're one of the only people who put up with her bullshit."

I scoff and relax into his body as he falls silent, clearly with his mind taking him places it shouldn't be. "What?" I whisper into the quiet hallway.

He lets out a sigh and before he's spoken a word, my heart is already breaking. "I shouldn't have done that job. Rivers was right. It wasn't urgent. I could have waited until after school and taken you two home first, but I didn't want to wait and I hated the thought of you looking at me that way you always do when I say I have to go."

"Noah," I sigh. "This isn't your fault."

"I know," he tells me. "But my actions are what put all three of you in that car. If it wasn't for me, Rivers probably would have fucked around with Alyssa all afternoon and you two would have been with me. The whole thing could have been avoided."

"Stop," I murmur, pressing my lips to his. "This isn't on you. There are a million different possibilities in play here. Rivers could have taken the back streets. Alyssa could have walked home. Hell, Tully and I could have walked. This. Is. Not. On. You. Got it?"

"Just because you say it with your sharp little attitude, doesn't make it true," he tells me.

"You're impossible," I smile.

"And you're going to give me a heart attack one day. I swear, I never want to get a call like that ever again. It will be a cold day in hell when something like that happens again."

"Shit, I don't know about a cold day in hell, but it was definitely cold in that car with Alyssa there. I mean, fuck.

Tully nearly pulled out her hair."

We sit and talk for a while and before I know it, the murmurs from the opposite side of the wall seem to have slowed down. Noah helps me to my feet and we head back in the room to find Rivers laying down in Tully's bed, holding her close while being as gentle as he can, giving her exactly what she needs to feel at ease.

Noah practically forces me back into my bed before sitting at the end of it, talking to Rivers about the state of his car and from what I gather, his insurance will cover it, but it will be more like a payout rather than getting another one. I guess he'll be back to searching for his dream car. It's a shame. He didn't even get to drive it for a whole week.

A knock sounds at the door and the boys' eyes fall towards it as the door handle turns. I don't bother, we've been bombarded by doctors and nurses since we first ended up in this hell hole. I'm sure it's just another one coming to check up on us.

The door begins to creep open and the second I see Rocko step over the threshold with a cheap as fuck looking bouquet of flowers in his hands and an awkward expression on his face, all hell breaks loose.

It all happens so quickly. One minute, Rivers is holding Tully as though she the most precious thing this world has ever created, the next, Rocko has him up against the wall, threatening to beat the shit out of him for hurting his girl and then having the balls to climb in bed with her.

He doesn't fight back or even reply, and when Noah goes to take a move, Rivers shakes his head. Not a moment later, he storms out the door while everybody watches on in silence.

CHAPTER 19

I sit in my bed, playing a game of 'Go Fish' with Aria, scowling as she continues to cheat, though the kicker is, she doesn't even realize she's doing it, nor does she understand what I'm trying to explain every time she does it. She must think I'm a real sore loser.

It's day three of being home from the hospital, and so far, it's driving me insane. I feel perfectly fine to go to school and be part of the world again, but Dad and Noah are both insisting that I finish the week off at home.

It's so freaking annoying.

If they were in my position, they'd be out of bed in a heartbeat, yet I feel like I have two broody, asshole, guard dogs keeping me locked in my ivory tower. It completely sucks.

Don't get me wrong, they have a little merit to their asshole ways. I ended up with a nasty headache after spending the day cleaning the house out of pure boredom, my body is still covered head to toe in cuts and bruises, and apparently, there are a few too many rumors going around school claiming they know the truth about the crash. Some people are even saying that the crash was staged and that I actually just went apeshit on Tully in a pure rage because I'm a bitch like that.

Noah quickly set them straight, but it doesn't stop the chatter.

Tully is not impressed to still be laying helpless in the hospital bed. If I'm going insane here, then she must be going certifiably crazy over there. There's nothing Tully hates more than complying with someone else. Well, I guess this is kind of different as her own health and safety are in question and she's really in too much pain to do anything about it, but I swear, every time a nurse comes in and tells her to take her pills, she scowls up at them as though they are there to personally victimize her.

It's actually getting quite entertaining…that is until I was forced to go home and spend my days locked inside.

With Noah in school and Rivers…well, actually, I don't really know where the hell he is. No one's really seen him much since the day Rocko came into the hospital. He apparently stopped in at the hospital to see Tully when no one else was around, checking that she's healing alright, but apart from that…nothing. Noah says he's not at school and he's not been at their house, so with no one really knowing too much about his personal life, we have no fucking idea where he's been. My guess is that the guilt is eating him up, but he needs to work out how to let go of it because shit like that will do more harm than good.

So yeah, with Noah in school and Rivers wherever the hell he is, I've basically been stranded here. Dad and Noah have flat out refused to allow me behind the wheel of a car so I've been forced to stay home, unable to actually go and physically check on Tully. Noah ensures me she's doing fine, but it's not the same when I can't see her for myself.

We've been texting each other nonstop. There's only so much Netflix I can watch to keep myself entertained. Tully is mostly alright because she's got her Kindle, but I haven't quite fallen in love with reading in the same, ridiculously obsessive way she has. I've read two books since the crash but not the impressive six that Tully has torn through. I swear, she probably sees all this as some kind of chance to make a dent in her 'To Be Read' pile.

Aria sees the card I pick up and instantly takes it out of my hands, adding it to the group of at least nine cards in her hand. "I win," she yells.

"Really, now?" I grumble, looking over the cards she puts down on the bed before her.

She doesn't have one single match.

"Uh huh," she grins.

"Damn it, that's four times in a row. How are you so good at this?"

She beams up at me as though I just handed her Christmas day on a silver platter, though, now that I think about it, she's probably never celebrated Christmas in a true merry way before. We'll have to remember to put a little extra effort this year.

We've started giving up on the whole big Christmas thing since I've gotten older, neither of us needs that extra effort, but now with Aria, we can bring back my childhood. Though this time, we won't have a mom sitting around, ignoring us the whole time. It'll be great.

Shit, Dad's going lose his mind when I suggest decorating the house. I can't exactly picture him willingly climbing up on the roof to hang a ten foot Santa Claus and his sleigh, but I'll twist Noah's finger until he agrees to do it instead. I might even add some lights and a nativity scene that has music playing.

Damn, this is going to be an expensive Christmas.

"Hey," dad's rumbly voice says from my bedroom doorway. We both look up to see him leaning against my open door frame, looking in on us as though we're the sole reason for his being. "Time to get ready for school, Squirt."

"Nooooo," Aria whines, drawing it out. "That's not fair. Henley doesn't have to go to school. Can't I stay at home too?"

"Henley was in an accident," Dad fires back.

I poke my tongue out at my sister, teasing her before deciding to give dad a little help. "Don't think I'm staying home on purpose. It's boring spending all day in bed. Trust me, you'll hate it, and besides, I thought you loved going to school?"

"I do," she tells me with big puppy dog eyes.

"Then what's the problem?" dad questions.

"I want to stay with Henley," she pouts. "If she's not allowed to go to her school, can she come to school with me? I promise, my teacher will be nice."

She turns those big puppy dog eyes on dad and for a moment I actually worry that I'm about to be sent to Kindergarten to get a refresher course of my 'ABC's'. "Geez," I tell her. "I wish I had those big blue eyes like you do, I would have gotten away with murder as a kid."

"You did get away with murder," he murmurs before letting out a sigh and rounding up Aria. "Come on, kid. Go get ready. You can play with Henley after school." He tells her. "I might even let her pick you up."

I roll my eyes as Aria sucks in an excited breath. Dad and I both know that's a little white lie to get her moving. There's no way he's letting me out of here. I'll probably be stuck in this bed until I'm thirty, especially if you take into account that he only just stopped checking over my scars from when I got jumped. I can't wait to see how he's going to handle the next few months.

Aria climbs off my bed, knocking all the cards to the ground and running off, leaving me to clean them up, which I probably won't do. I expect dad to go after her, to help get her breakfast sorted, but when he hovers in my doorway, I find myself glancing up at him and silently watching him.

Dad lets out a sigh and walks forward into my room,

pulling up my desk chair and spinning it to face me. "How are you feeling, Squish?" he questions, looking nervous as shit.

"Fine. I'm good to get out of here though."

"Bullshit," he grumbles. "You look like you volunteered to climb under my truck and let me roll over you a few times."

"It's not that bad," I tell him, scoffing at his exaggeration. "It's just a little bruising."

"It's more than that and you know it," he says, being one of the only people on this planet who refuses to take my shit. Noah being another.

"What's going on, dad?" I question, getting down to the nitty-gritty. I mean. He's not sitting in my room like this because he wants to braid my hair. "Why do you look like you're about to hurl?"

He cringes. "That obvious, huh?"

"Dad," I prompt.

He lets out a loud breath before raising his eyes to meet mine. "There's something I've been wanting to talk to you about," he starts as my brows pull down. "I've been battling with myself over this decision for the past few years, but now with Aria here and considering you're not far off eighteen, I think it's the right time to tell you and I wanted to say something before you start putting the pieces of the puzzle together for yourself."

I watch him cautiously, wondering if he just started talking jibberish because I seriously have no clue what he's talking about. "What puzzle? What are you talking about?"

"It's about your mom," he warns.

My back straightens, instantly on alert as hundreds of unwelcome thoughts start swirling through my mind. Every last one of them to do with Aria. "What about her?" I question, feeling a wall come down within me, preparing myself for the worst. That bitch better not be coming to take my sister.

Dad rubs a hand over his face, clearly letting me know that whatever he's got to say isn't easy. "Since Aria's been here, I'm sure you've been noticing a few slight…differences."

Huh? What the fuck is he going on about?

"How do you mean?" I question. "There's been heaps of difference. Our whole world is different now."

"No, no," he rushes in. "I don't mean those differences. I mean differences between the two of you."

"Ummm…what?"

"Your appearances. She has my blonde curls while you have a dark, golden color and straight hair."

"She has your eyes," I add.

"Exactly," he murmurs."

"What are you talking about, Dad?" I ask, not liking where this is going at all. "Are you trying to tell me that you're not my dad because if you are, you can walk straight out of here. I'm so not prepared for that kind of shit."

"No, no, no," he says, holding up a hand, hoping that can somehow slow down my thought process. "What I'm saying is that she's not your mom."

"What?" I grunt, blinking a few times as I watch his features. He's got to be fucking with me, right? Not my mom. Bullshit. That has got to be some twisted joke to follow up my 'dad' comment. "Are you on crack? What the fuck are you talking about? How can she not be my mom?" I question as I start to ramble, wondering if I need to knock on his head to check that he's got a brain in there. "Every single photo we have of me as a baby has her in it. I mean, were you even there? Are you remembering this correctly?"

"Henley, if you could give me two seconds to speak, I'll be able to explain."

I shake my head. "No, this is too…no. Not possible. I look just like her."

He arches a brow. "Do you though?"

I stop for a second. "Of course, I do," I say a little slower than I had before as I truly think about it. She's blonde and blue eyed just like me, but her blue is more of a greyish blue where mine is a stormy ocean blue. She has a natural wave to her hair and is a short ass. I'm leggy with straight hair. I don't resemble her features and I sure as hell don't have the same mannerisms.

Dad's claim starts to have little merit. "You need to start explaining," I tell him as my world begins crumbling around me. What the hell could he mean that she's not my mom? She was there from the very start. This doesn't make sense. Of course, she's my mom. I mean, I'm not exactly thrilled about it, I didn't exactly hit the mommy jackpot, but it is what it is.

Dad clears his throat, preparing himself for the explanation of a lifetime and though I know I should be paying complete attention, all I can do is repeat four little words over and over again in my head. 'She's not your mom.' 'She's not your mom.' 'She's not your mom.'

"As you know," Dad starts as a shade of green seeps into his features. "I'm not exactly one for having a woman in my life."

I scoff.

"I've always been this way," he tells me. "Before you were born, I was living life to the fullest, or what I thought was the fullest back then. I was young. I was partying every night, staying out drinking, getting high. I hated the thought of being tied down to a woman, but then, I liked women, a lot of women."

"Dad," I grunt, scrunching up my face in distaste.

"What I'm trying to say is that I had spent a night with a woman, and nine months later, she's knocking on my door with a beautiful little girl in her arms. The same as what happened with Aria, so you can believe my shock when that happened," he chuckles to himself before shaking his head. "I'm getting off track, but Squish, you blew me the hell away. You were only a few days old and your mom…your real mom said she couldn't do it. She wasn't fit to be a mom so she handed you over and I haven't seen her since."

My mouth drops open. "Are you shitting me, right now? This couldn't be true. I don't believe it."

"Henley, why would I lie about this? I don't like the idea of hurting you, but with Aria here, you were soon going to realize how different you both are, how you don't have the same features."

"I have noticed that and I just figured I got more of mom."

"And you never questioned how you hardly resemble her, either?"

"But I just... I never questioned it because I never had a reason to doubt it."

Dad lets out a deep sigh. "I'm sorry, Squish. I know this isn't easy to take in."

"Not easy to take in?" I shriek before mimicking his tone. "Morning Squish, hope you're feeling better. Oh, by the way, I've been lying to you your whole life."

Dad's eyes nervously flick towards the door. "Keep your voice down," he scolds, not appreciating my attitude, but what did he expect? He knows me well enough by now to know that when in doubt, my sarcastic flare comes out. Hell, I know I certainly got that from him.

"You have to understand the reasons I've kept this from you," he tells me. "We had a happy life with your mom. It wasn't the best but it was good. I had no reason to rock your world with the truth and it didn't matter because no matter what, you were my child and you were loved."

"But I wasn't," I tell him. "I've had two mothers walk out on me."

"You can't look at it like that. Your real mom... she wasn't your mom at all. She's just some woman who shares your DNA, and Kelly, Aria's mom, she did her best, but in the end, she just couldn't cut being a mom. That much is clear with the way she failed Aria. You are better off without them both and you know that. Deep down in your heart, you know that."

My head drops as my head starts to ache. This is too much.

"So, you waited nearly eighteen years to tell me the truth?"

"Does it make a difference?" he questions. "Knowing that Kelly isn't your real mom? Knowing that you don't share the DNA of a junkie?"

"I guess," I mutter, "but all that does is tell me that I share the DNA of a woman who wasn't strong enough to be my mom and that the very first thing to ever happen to me was being given up by the one person who's supposed to love me the most."

"Don't say that," he tells me. "It's taken me a while to come to this realization, but what it means is that your mom, your real biological mom is probably one of the strongest people I've ever met."

"This has got to be good," I grumble, showing off my award-winning sarcasm again.

Dad ignores me. "How many people do you know have what it takes to admit that they're not good enough? That someone else could do a better job at raising their child than they could? Because that's exactly what she did. She knew she wasn't going to give you a good life so she handed you over, knowing that you had a better shot with me. Every single day I thank her for making such a difficult decision. Now, I know you don't have fancy cars and expensive clothes, but I did everything I could to make sure I gave you the best possible life."

"I'm not complaining about my life, dad. I've had a great life. I love my home and the people I have around me. I have everything I could have asked for, it's just…I guess it's a lot to take in," I tell him. "I mean, who is this woman? Does she even look like me?"

Dad smiles. "Her name is Gina and you're the spitting

image of her," he tells me. "I haven't seen her since the day she came knocking on my door, she would have been around twenty years old, but you look just like she did that day. It gets me every time you walk by me."

"Really?" I ask. "Was she at least…I don't know, a nice, decent person?"

He shrugs his shoulders. "Couldn't really tell you, Squish, but I like to think she would have been tough, just as you are. She didn't strike me as a woman who would take shit from anyone."

"So, Kelly?" I question, shaking my head, still trying to work it all out.

"She's nothing to you. I met her when you were five months old and we instantly hit it off. She thought the fact that I had a baby was adorable and by the time you started talking, you were calling her 'Mom.' We didn't think to correct you and from there, it just stuck. She became your mom and you, as a child, absolutely loved her."

"I guess that didn't last long," I mutter wondering how this is going to affect my abandonment issues. I mean, two moms abandoned me. That shit is going to sit inside my head and fester until I can't take it anymore. This is the kind of stuff that would put the sanest person in therapy and considering how screwed up I already am, I'll probably end up in a strait jacket.

My mind swirls, trying to picture an older version of me, some stranger that apparently gave me life. I hope when the time comes that when I have a baby, I'll be a lot stronger than she was. Dad thinks she's strong for being able to admit that, but I can't find it within myself to agree.

She pushed me aside. She didn't even give me a chance.

Strong is taking on the challenge and rising up, being the best parent you can be. Struggle through the hard times and love through the good. Nowhere in the strong handbook does it say cop out and give away your flesh and blood to some unexpecting guy that you met once, probably in a shady bar.

What the hell does that say about me? I'm the result of a one night stand.

I look up at dad with an urge to know more about this woman, a need to know where she came from, what she's like, and if I share any of her qualities other than just her looks. I guess I need to know what kind of person I have the potential to become. "Do you know her last name or where she is?"

Dad's lips thing into a hard line. "You don't want to go looking for her, do you?"

"Why not?"

"She gave you up, Squish," he says softly. "She's not magically going to want to have some sort of relationship with you. I haven't moved in eighteen years. She knows where to find you and has never come looking."

I shake my head. "It's not that," I tell him, struggling to find a way to describe what's going through my head. "I just want to know what she's like. You know, figure out what I've missed out on."

Dad considers me for a moment. "Are you sure?" he questions. "I don't want you getting your hopes up over this woman."

"I'm sure, Dad. I just want to know who she is."

"Ok," he says, letting out a sigh. "Her last name is Rivers. Gina Rivers."

"Rivers?" I grunt.

The front door of our home slams open and both dad and I jump to our feet. Who the fuck was that? "Aria?" Dad yells before darting for my bedroom door, assuming she's just escaped.

He's stopped in the doorway by Noah who all but barges through, forcing Dad back in as he gapes at me. "Why the fuck aren't you answering your phone?" Noah demands.

"What?" I grunt. "I have more important things going on right now."

"What the hell is going on?" Dad questions, not pleased about the intrusion into our home.

Noah cringes at Dad before turning his attention on me. "There's a video of you and it just got sent through the whole fucking school."

"What?" I say slowly, confused about what he's talking about.

Dad's eyes practically bulge out of his head. "What fucking video?" he roars. "If you made a fucking sex tape, Henley. So help me God."

"No," Noah rushes out, hopefully to throw a little light on the situation. "It's a video of when she got hurt," he says with a cringe. "The first time with Monica and Candice. When you were jumped."

"What?" I shriek, not giving a shit that I haven't been able to come up with any other words to convey what's going on in my head. I all but dive across my bed, grabbing my phone off the bedside table and ripping it off the charger.

I'd put it on silent last night and clearly, that was a mistake.

The screen lights up to at least fifty messages, all from kids at school. I search through them and scroll straight past the missed calls and urgent texts from Noah until I find the original message that comes with the video attachment.

I open the video as dad watches over my shoulder.

The video starts and the first thing I see is Monica's back before my voice comes shooting out of the speaker on my phone as a broken cry for help. "No, no, no, no, no," I say, repeating myself over and over again as the last piece of dignity I held onto escapes me. Noah had said this was sent through the whole school so literally everyone I know has witnessed my weakest moment.

"Who sent this out?" I beg, desperate for answers.

Noah shakes his head, not wanting to give me the information that's on the end of his tongue, but the answer is crystal clear. "I'll give you one guess."

"Monica," I sigh, looking down at the girl in the video, pummeling her fists into my body over and over again.

I should have known. Monica gets her kicks by keeping dirt on her victims. I literally just took her down for this shit. I found every last piece of dirt she was hiding and destroyed it. How could I have been so stupid to assume she wouldn't have something on me?

The video goes on and on until my phone is ripped out of my hand and thrown across my room, splintering against the wall into a hundred little pieces. "Someone is going to fucking pay for that," Dad promises before storming out of my bedroom.

I storm out right behind him, not giving a shit that I'm not dressed and head straight for the entryway table.

I grab the keys to the old pick up and reach for the door when Noah grabs my arm, pulling me back. "Where the fuck do you think you're going?"

"I'm fucking dealing with this, that's what," I tell him. "Either come with me or not, but whether or not you're by my side, I'm going to fucking end this. She's gone too far."

Noah pulls the keys out of my hand and tosses them back on the table. "Fine," he says. "But there's no way in hell you're driving. Go get some proper clothes on and I'll meet you out front."

Thirty seconds later, I'm out the door, ready to knock some fucking heads together.

CHAPTER 20

I storm through the school just moments after the first bell sounded with Noah right by my side. We sat in the car in absolute silence as he raced towards the school. I resisted telling him to hurry it up and drive as though he was on a racetrack while he resisted asking me about my, 'I have more important things going on right now' comment.

Students still linger in the halls, but the majority of them are already in homeroom. The lingering ones though, they get one look at the expression on my face, most likely having already seen the video, they take in the deathly fury radiating out of Noah and they scram like little bitches. The cuts and bruises covering me, only serving to help my cause.

Nobody wants to be around for this. There was the Spencer drama a few weeks ago and compared to this shit, that was just child's play. People are more than happy to sit around and enjoy that show, but this…this is fucking war.

This was taking a direct hit against their queen, trying to take me down. Every last person who walks these halls knows that if they even accidentally stand in my way right

207

now, they'll be going down right alongside the bitch who dared wrong me.

Within seconds of us walking through the doors of Haven Falls Private, the hallways are a fucking ghost town.

"Game face," Noah reminds me in a low murmur, assuming that my emotions will get the best of me and I'll fuck it all up. If only he knew about the baby mumma drama, he probably wouldn't bother with the reminder. My game face has been on since dad walked through my bedroom door this morning.

I don't respond, but it's not like he was expecting me to.

"You ready for this?" he questions with a slight hesitance in his tone, though anyone listening in right now would never be able to detect it.

"Try and fucking stop me, Noah," I warn. "I'm seeing this through."

His chin lowers, and again, no one but me would be able to decipher it. It's not only his 'go ahead,' but it's his way of telling me to take point. This guy beside me right now, this isn't Noah Cage, my boyfriend and the guy who puts up with me teasing him about pink dildoes in his bedside table. This is Noah Fucking Cage, King of Haven Falls, Pack Leader and most feared badass around.

And that right there was the fucking King handing the reigns to his Queen.

The only thing that feels wrong about this is not having Tully and Rivers here with us. Without a doubt, they would know what's going on. I'm sure I scrolled past a shitload of texts from Tully before looking at the video this morning, but I'll call her later. Hell, I'm already out of my prison so I may as well head straight to the hospital and spend the day with her after this.

Rivers though, I can't possibly understand why he isn't here right now. That isn't how we work. When a member of our pack needs something, we run. That's just how it is, how it's always going to be, so unless he's in shit of his own, I couldn't even begin to imagine what he could be doing right now. I have a feeling Noah will have words with him about this later though.

Those two just haven't been the same lately and it's really tearing at me. I get the fight in the hospital; both their emotions were riding high and I can imagine that Noah's still a bit pissed about Rivers breaking Tully's heart despite the fact that he says otherwise. Now's not the time to dwell on it though, I'm here to do a job and a damn good one at that.

We come to the end of the hallway with either a left or right turn and it hits me that I have no fucking clue where the hell Monica's homeroom. I don't want to stop. My feet refuse to quit moving so when Noah murmurs a quick, "Barrett's room," I find myself finally seeing the one good thing that came out of Noah dating the girl for all that time.

I turn to the left and head straight for Mr. Barrett's room. It's towards the end of this hallway and I don't doubt that by the time we get down there, she will already know that I'm coming.

The door to Barrett's room is closed and we don't waste a second storming through it. Barrett's head whips up from the papers on his desk and I see a scolding on his lips, but the second he realizes who stands at the door, he backs right down.

The teachers at this school aren't stupid. They know what's good for them and they know when the hell to back down. Times exactly like this.

A loud gasp sails through the class and my eyes instantly follow the sound.

Monica. Otherwise known as 'dead fucking meat.'

Her eyes widen as I zone in on her and without a doubt, she knows she's finished. Right now, she's breathing on borrowed time and I can't wait to bring her down. Again. Let's just hope she's smart enough to stay down this time.

She sits towards the back of the room, in the furthest corner which I distantly realize is the further space possible from the three cheerleaders who sit across the other side of the room. Smart move on her part, if only she was smart enough not to challenge me again.

I cut up the closest aisle while Noah walks across the front of the room, taking the other aisle, blocking her way if she were to run.

Fear eats at her and I should feel sick knowing just how happy that makes me, but I don't. I thrive on this shit, especially when it's because of bitches like this.

The closer I get, the straighter she sits.

Three steps. She starts shaking her head as others sitting around her begin to pull away, terrified of getting caught in the middle.

"No. No, I didn't…" Monica starts blabbering.

Two steps. She pulls back in her chair, her eyes flicking around the room in terror.

One step. She starts to rise, ready to make a break for it.

Too fucking late. The chance to run was after she jumped me, and she missed that shot by miles.

I rush in, slamming my hands down on either shoulder, forcing her back down into her chair. "I suggest you don't fucking move," I tell her.

Instinct has her fighting me off and the lesson Rivers had tried to teach me about thinking things through flies out the fucking window. I grab her by the back of the neck and slam her head down on the desk before me.

"I told you not to fucking move," I seethe as Noah stands back, completely allowing me to take control. "You sent out that video. Is this what you want? To bring me down in front of the whole school? Because you know how I love to fight back. I've already taken you down, don't think I won't do it again."

A thought flashes in my mind that I'm taking this too far and that it would be smart to back up a bit, but I can't seem to stop myself. The pain from dad's earlier revelation and the sting of watching myself on that video are too much for me too handle. My emotions are shot and I'm desperate to get to the bottom this.

I can't breathe. I need to see this through.

I need this to be over.

Monica sucks in a sharp breath as if only now realizing what a psycho bitch I can be. But hey, she's the one who turned me into this.

Her eyes flick up to Noah and I see a silent plea, hoping that whatever history they have together is enough for him to sweep this under the rug. His only response is to fold his arms over his wide chest and raise his chin as he looks down at her through narrowed eyes. He looks scary as fuck, but I don't blame him, this bitch just tried to hurt his queen.

Seeing that there's no hope for her with Noah and no help coming from the other students in the room, she starts to backpedal. "I didn't do it," she cries. "The video wasn't mine."

I scoff. "Yeah fucking right. Do you forget who the bitch in that video is? You forget that I was there?" I squish her face harder into the desk. "You forget that it was my ribs you kicked over and over again?" I demand.

"After the blackmailing shit with the cheerleaders, you fucking expect me to think you didn't organize someone to record that to use against me?"

"I did," she yells out. "But I didn't send it. I swear."

Noah steps forward, slamming his hand down on the table, making us all jump. "Whose phone was it recorded on?"

"Tiffany's," she rushes out.

A gasp is heard from across the room and I look across to find Tiffany sitting up against the wall, her hands raised in innocence. "I filmed it," she admits, too terrified to even dream of lying about it. "I sent it straight to Monica afterward and deleted it off my phone. I didn't want the evidence."

"Henley saved your fucking ass a few weeks ago and you didn't think to do the same for her?"

Tiffany shrugs. "Sorry, but Henley offered to do it to get me on her side. I didn't owe her anything."

"You didn't owe the girl who didn't rat you out for jumping her and finding the dirt that Monica was using against you?" he questions. "You're fucked up, but don't you worry, we'll deal with you in time."

Fear flashes in her eyes as Noah turns back to Monica. Tiffany is a problem we can deal with another day, right now, Monica needs to be put back in place.

"Looks like the spotlight is back on you," I murmur, deathly low to Monica, releasing her head and sitting on the edge of her desk, so close she has to crane her neck to see me. "Tell me, I'd love to hear your side of the story."

She instantly starts shaking her head, tears springing in her eyes. "I swear, I didn't do it."

"Says the girls who lied about…well, everything."

"I swear," she repeats, looking between me and Noah. "I've done some fucked up things over the past six months that I'm not proud of. Like seriously fucked up, but I've learned my lesson and kept my head down. I just want to graduate. Please, you've got to believe me."

"And you've got to understand how fucking hard it is to do that," I tell her. "You see, literally all of the evidence is pointing your way. You were the brains behind me being jumped. You're the sad bitch who keeps blackmail to get yourself off. You're the one who had the video. What am I supposed to think?"

"I know it looks bad, but I didn't do it." The tears start to fall and for the first time, I start doubting myself. "I swear, Henley. It wasn't me. I haven't been to any fucking parties and I haven't tried to climb my way back up. I just want senior year to finish so I can get the fuck out of here. You've already ruined what little chance I had at having any sort of social status, so what could I possibly gain by sending out that video?"

I narrow my eyes on her. She has a fucking point.

"There are bitches all around this school who are dying to take you down. They all want what you have," she continues, quickly glancing at Noah. "You have him, the grand fucking prize. You have the respect of the whole school and the status every girl wants. Anyone of them could have gained something by sending out that video, but not me. All I would have gained is a fucking smackdown. Lucky me, huh?"

"So, who the fuck sent it?" I demand. "It was on your fucking phone."

She shrugs her shoulders. "I don't know," she says. "Anyone could have gotten it. Tiffany emailed it. Despite her deleting it off her phone, it would have still been in her sent emails. Someone could have hacked her phone, or mine, or hell, the fucking cloud. Everything stays on the fucking cloud."

"Uhhh…" a nervous voice says from behind me. I whip around to face the designated school nerd. His name is Simon and he's in my Biology class and despite the fact that I'm a fellow science nerd, I've never talked to him before.

My eyes narrow on him and he instantly snaps his mouth shut. He either has balls of steel or a death wish for interrupting my interrogation; either way, I'm going to find out which.

"Can I help you?" I demand, momentarily forgetting just how bitchy I can sound.

"I…I…I."

"Spit it out," Noah growls.

Simon swallows, his eyes flicking back. "I, uh, I could hack into the school network and find out where the blast originated from."

I raise a brow. "You can do that?"

"Well, yes. It's not exactly hard," he says, spinning the phone on his desk around and showing me the video. He clicks into the sender's details. "It was sent from a school email."

213

Noah snatches Simon's phone off his desk and looks closer at it. "How the hell do you know that's a school address?"

"I…I just do," Simon says.

"Well," I say turning back to Monica with a cocky smirk. "I guess we'll find out who sent it after all."

Noah hands the phone back to Simon and after a beat of him not doing anything, Noah grunts. "What the fuck are you waiting for? Find out who sent it."

"Oh," Simon says, sucking in a breath. "I need a computer."

"Right, then," I say, standing and stepping around to his desk. "Lead the way."

Simon looks back at Mr. Barrett who studiously ignores him, not wanting anything to do with this. I watch Simon swallow and nod, probably cursing himself for getting himself involved.

As we walk towards the door, I refrain from smirking when Noah takes the long route, passing slowly by Tiffany's desk and making her shrink back into the wall, terrified of what's going to come.

As we step out into the hallway, Simon leads the way. He walks before us as Noah takes my hand. "Are you ok?"

"Think so," I murmur. "I just want to get to the bottom of this." I let out a sigh. "Call me crazy, but I don't think Monica had anything to do with it, you know apart from being the star of the show and having Tiffany record it."

"I think you're right," he murmurs into the too quiet hallway. "I just can't work out who the fuck would have done it."

"That's the million dollar question," I grumble to myself.

I hear someone walking quickly from the opposite end of the hallway and spin around, ready to take down whoever dares come at me now. "Henley," Principal Evans calls out. He jogs a little to catch up with us. "I heard you were here."

"News travels fast, huh?" I murmur.

"Yes, look. I know you're not supposed to be back at school yet, so I wanted to catch you before you left," he says. "I won't keep you long, but I've just had a...colorful conversation with your dad. He informed me of what's been going on this morning and I wanted you to know that we will get to the bottom of this. A full investigation will be held and the girls responsible for hurting you will be punished."

"Thanks, but we handle our own drama."

A dissatisfied look pierces across his face before he tries to right himself, remembering that despite my attitude, I'm the victim here. "No matter how you decide to handle it, it's now a school matter as the video involves my students and has been spread throughout my school."

"I said that we-"

"Henley," Noah mutters beside me before looking up at Evans. "Thanks."

Principal Evans nods and realizing that's the best he's going to get; he turns and walks away.

"What the hell was that?" I demand, giving Simon a nudge to get him moving again.

"It was principal Evans finally stepping up and doing something about the bullshit that goes down in this school. Candice and Monica have been dealt with by us, but they're still walking through these halls every day. We might have taken away their social status, but have they really been punished for what they did? They deserve to suffer for putting their hands on you."

"Yeah, but-"

"But nothing. It is what it is. Deal with it," he tells me as we follow Simon into the computer lab.

He instantly sits down as Noah and I hover behind him, watching every move he makes. Simon powers up the computer and I impatiently wait while my phone burns a hole in my pocket, knowing that Tully is waiting for something from me.

The computer finally gets up and running and I watch in

awe as Simon's fingers move across the keyboard like lightning. He instantly hacks into the school network and starts doing something that I can't even keep up with. "Are you able to somehow remove the video from all the people who got it?"

"Ahhh, maybe," he says. "A lot of people got that blast. I could, but it'd take a while. I'm not exactly working for the FBI. I just play around."

"Can you try?"

"I'll see what I can do," he says. "But I can't guarantee that the people who have already seen it, haven't forward it on to other people."

Damn it. I was worried about that. I need to know for sure.

"Don't worry, babe," Noah says, placing his hand on my lower back and spreading his fingers. "We'll work on that. Can we just figure out who the hell sent it first?"

"Yeah," I say, watching anxiously.

The conversation falls silent as we watch over Simon's shoulder. "Alright," he says after a little while. "I can see that the email was sent from computer five," he says, quickly glancing across the room to the offending computer before getting back to it. "It was sent at 8:17am this morning," he says slowly, piecing together the information as he's getting it. "And it was logged in with the student ID – 7258."

"Who the fuck is that?" Noah grunts as I take hold of his hand, giving it a squeeze.

"Hold on," Simon murmurs, concentrating on the computer as he goes into the student records. "Alright, student ID – 7258 is..." he sucks in a breath, his back straightening. "Oh, shit."

"What?" Noah demands.

I hear Simon swallow. "7258 is Rivers," he tells us. "Rivers sent the blast."

ABOUT THE AUTHOR

Sheridan Anne is a wife to a smart-ass husband, Mumma to two beautiful girls, twin sister, daughter, and friend who lives in beautiful Australia. Sheridan writes both romance and young adult fantasy books on a variety of topics and can be found on most days with her family or writing during nap time. To find out more or to simply say 'hello', connect with her on Facebook.

www.facebook.com/SheridanAnneAuthor/

SERIES BY SHERIDAN ANNE

The Guard Trilogy

Kings of Denver

Denver Royalty

Rebels Advocate

Broken Hill High

Haven Falls

Made in the USA
Monee, IL
13 November 2019

16731040R00129